MW00985934

Trapped by a wizard's spell...

As Randal and Walter watched, the glowing column grew into a cylinder about a yard across and three yards high. A man in chain mail and a closed helmet stepped out of the cylinder.

"Look outside," said Randal, pointing to the tent flap. A line of blue fire ran past the entrance. "Another magic circle . . ."

More men came out of the pillar of golden light as he spoke. They began passing the chests of gold back into the portal. Just as the last chest was being loaded, one of the men looked up and spotted Randal.

Randal felt a sudden wrench as magic surged out from the pillar of gold. The light flared up like a bonfire—bright, blinding. He shielded his eyes with his forearm. Then, abruptly, the light ceased.

"That was a good trick, Randy," Walter's voice came to him. "Now will you please tell me where we are?"

"You mean you don't know?" came a voice in the dark. "You're in the dungeons of Bell Castle . . ."

CIRCLE OF MAGIC

THE WIZARD'S CASTLE

Debra Doyle and James D. Macdonald
illustrated by Judith Mitchell

To Gentle Jane, an inspiration to us all,
and Amy, patron of the arts

This edition published in 2000.

Originally published under the title *Circle of Magic: The Prisoners of Bell Castle*.

Copyright © 1990 by Troll Communications L.L.C.

All rights reserved. No part of this book may be reproduced or utilized in any
form or by any means, electronic or mechanical, including photocopying,
recording, or by any information storage and retrieval system, without
written permission from the publisher.

Cover photography by Steven Dolce.

Printed in the United States of America.

10 9 8 7 6 5 4 3 2 1

I.

The Castle

"I TELL YOU, Randy, this is one journey I'll be glad to see over and done with."

Randal of Doun—a sturdy, brown-haired youth in the dark, hooded robe of a journeyman wizard—turned in the saddle and regarded his cousin Walter for a moment before replying.

Walter himself, at a little past the age of twenty, was only four years Randal's senior, but he was already a knight, and the long sword at his side was no child's toy. He and Randal had ridden most of the day in watchful silence, while the pack train behind them wound its way through the hills of northeastern Brecelande.

"We shouldn't run into any more trouble on the road," Randal said, in reply to the question Walter hadn't asked aloud. "I didn't see anything last night, when I used the scrying-spell to look ahead."

Randal didn't blame his cousin for being worried. Six chests full of gold—borrowed by a lord in Brecelande to pay for a campaign he planned to fight—made dangerous baggage in a land already at war. He considered the road ahead for a moment, then shrugged and added, "Of course, nothing's certain. We may have enemies who are spelled against magical detection, or we might find ourselves caught by a danger that's only now coming into being, or we . . ."

"If you're trying to sound cheerful," came a light alto voice from behind Randal, "it isn't working."

The voice belonged to the slightly built girl in boy's clothing who rode next to Prince Vespian's paymaster. The girl wore a jaunty cap of green felt on her short black curls, and carried a lute slung over her shoulder in a leather case. Beside her, the paymaster sat hunched glumly in his saddle—the farther Prince Vespian's gold had come from its native southlands, the longer the paymaster's face had grown, until now he almost never smiled or even spoke at all.

Sir Walter turned and grinned at the lute player. "I'd sooner have honest uncertainty than false security, Demoiselle Lys," he said. "And I'd hate to lose everything at the last moment. Baron Ector trusted me to bring the gold to him at Bell Castle, with no glory-seeking along the way."

"Why do they call it Bell Castle?" Lys asked curiously.

"You'll hear for yourself soon enough," Walter promised. "The baron's camp is just ahead."

2

The pack train crested another hill as the knight spoke, and Randal saw an open plain filled with tents and pavilions. He frowned a little at the sight: Even from this distance, he could see that part of the field had once been a village and plowed farmland. The villagers—the men and women who grew Bell Castle's food, and shared its protection—were nowhere in sight; Randal supposed that they had gone into the castle for safety, much as the peasants at Doun turned to Walter's father in time of trouble.

Randal looked up from the low-lying plain to where more hills began to rise from the valley floor. The castle stood in isolation at the top of a steep slope on a spur of bare granite. Blocks of the same gray stone formed the castle's walls and its two great towers, one higher than the other, rising above the central keep.

"Well, Randy," said Sir Walter, "that's Bell Castle. What do you think of it?"

"I don't think I've ever seen a fortress so strong," said Randal honestly. "Does your Baron Ector really expect to take this place?"

Sir Walter cast a practiced eye over the camp on the plain below. "A thousand foot soldiers, and about five hundred mounted men—plus mercenaries, and the gold to pay them. Yes, I'd say my lord Baron is serious."

"Who exactly is Baron Ector?" Randal asked.

"Baron Ector of Wirrell," Walter replied, "is a war-leader of some note. He has a quarrel with another lord who holds land in these parts, including Bell Castle. What the castle itself holds, I'm not cer-

3

tain—it's not the largest of Lord Fess's castles, or the most important—but Baron Ector is determined to break it open and bring out the prize within."

Randal felt a chill run down his spine. He knew the name of Lord Fess. When a stolen artifact of power from Fess's treasure room had come into Randal's unwilling possession, Fess's men had chased him and Lys from Cingestoun to Widsegard in an attempt to get it back.

He glanced at the girl. She looked back at him, and shrugged. "We'd better hope the baron wins," was all she said.

As she spoke, the deep tolling of a massive bell came from the castle across the plain. The bell's dark, booming voice sent a feeling of powerful magic washing over Randal, which faded but did not entirely vanish as the echoes of the bell-note died.

"Bell Castle," he said. "Now I understand the name."

Walter nodded. "The castle-folk ring it once every hour, day and night. It's said no enemy can take the castle so long as that bell hangs in the top-most tower."

Magic, thought Randal. *And strong, too, from the feel of it. Once we're settled down, I'll have to look about and see what other spells the lord of the castle has in place.*

As the last echoes of the bell died away, the pack train started down the slope toward the plain. A group of mounted men rode toward them out of the camp ahead. As the troop came closer, Randal heard Lys give a shout of recognition.

4

"Look, Randy!" she cried out. "It's Sir Guillaume!"

Randal looked more closely at the oncoming riders, and saw that she spoke true. The horseman in the lead carried a shield emblazoned with three intertwined rings, the device of Sir Guillaume of Hernefeld. The last time Randal had seen that device had been in Tattinham, on the day of the great tournament there—a day when his cousin Walter had almost died, struck down from behind during a moment of truce.

Sir Guillaume spurred forward. "Sir Walter!" he called. "I'm glad to see you—I haven't heard of you all year! I was afraid you might be dead, after that wound you took."

Walter shook his head. "No, not dead—although the quest I was on afterward had me close enough to death a few times. But that's done with, and now I'm Baron Ector's man for this season. What brings you here?"

"The same as you," Guillaume replied. "I'm joined with the baron in his war on Lord Fess. And if you're with us, then we can't lose."

Walter said something modest in reply, and the pack train, now guarded by Guillaume's men as well as Walter's own, continued across the plain and into the center of the baron's camp. They stopped outside a large, airy pavilion decked out with banners. A heavyset man in his late forties stood outside the pavilion, a look of worry on his square, florid face. His expression lightened a little as Sir Walter and the others appeared.

5

"It's good you're here," he said to Walter. "Captain Dreikart and his troop of mercenaries were threatening to leave if they weren't paid soon."

"What we have here should keep them happy, my lord Baron," said Walter, with a nod toward the chests. "Prince Vespian's terms were more than generous."

"I see." Then the baron's eyebrows drew together in a frown at Randal's black robe. "Was the prince's wizard part of the bargain?"

"My cousin Randal isn't the prince's wizard," said Walter. "He was fostered with my family at Castle Doun."

"What was a son of Brecelande doing in Peda?" the baron asked.

Randal met the baron's gaze directly. "I'm a journeyman wizard, my lord. It's the custom for us to travel about in search of magical knowledge. I'd been studying with Prince Vespian's court wizard, and when the time came for me to journey on, I joined Sir Walter's pack train to help protect the gold."

"So you're not actually sworn to anybody," said the baron. He made a dissatisfied noise. "There are too many masterless men in this already . . . but I suppose it can't be helped. You, Sir Walter—are you willing to vouch for your cousin?"

"With my life," said Walter. "Randy's as trustworthy as the day is long."

"And the lute player there—how about her?" asked the baron. "She looks like a foreigner to me."

6

"Demoiselle Lys is from Occitania," Walter said. "But a truer friend you won't find anywhere."

"Well, let them camp with you and your men," said the baron. "Since you did such a good job of bringing the gold from Peda, I'm going to give you the responsibility for guarding it, as well—and if you're willing to have these two with you, I won't argue."

Later, with the gold safely stowed in the center of the camp, and Vespian's paymaster sleeping next to the locked chests, Walter and his little troop settled down for the night. Lys took her lute and began working over its many strings, bringing them back into tune after the day's travel, while Walter and Randal sat nearby and listened to the silvery jangle of sound. After a while, Walter lifted his gaze from the campfire's flames.

"So tell me, Randal—now that we've gotten the gold safely to Brecelande, what will you do next?"

Randal shrugged. "Travel, I suppose. Learn magic where I can. Go back to Tarnsberg someday, maybe, and study again with one of the masters there."

"But shouldn't you be doing more than just wandering about?" Walter asked curiously. "After all, pages become squires, and squires become knights—don't journeyman wizards someday become masters?"

"Not always," said Randal. "It's not that easy." He looked down at his hands, and shook his head. "I'm not really sure I want to claim mastery. Even a journeyman has too much power sometimes."

"I don't know," Walter said. "A man doesn't stay a squire forever. But I suppose it's different for wizards."

"Everything's different for wizards," said Randal. But his cousin's words made him uneasy just the same, and he fell silent, listening to Lys sing a ballad to the music of her lute.

> "Green is the hill, the elfin hill,
> And the birds fly high above.
> And I will go to the elfin hill
> And fly my hawk for Love."

The evening drew on, and eventually all the baron's camp inside the circle of sentries was wrapped in sleep. Randal lay curled in his journeyman's robe in Walter's tent, and counted the passing hours of the night with the ringing of the great bell.

At last he slept, and in his sleep he dreamed. In his dream he stood on a high plain, empty wherever he looked, with deep cracks running along the parched, hard earth. A hot wind blew across the barren ground, and whipped the ends of his hair against his cheeks and forehead.

He turned to look behind him, and saw that the plain was not entirely featureless after all: He stood before a broken heap of rock, a pile of gray stone that looked like part of a collapsed wall. A rosebush climbed up the side of the wall, its thorny vines holding fast to the ancient stonework.

Randal looked again, and saw that the rose was

not the only plant that grew over the broken stone. A brier grew out of the dry soil at the wall's base, and twined its brambles among the leaves and blossoms of the rosebush. The roses covered the ruined wall like a tapestry of petals—white roses below, near the roots, and red ones nearer the top, where the brier joined the rosebush in its push toward the sun.

Randal walked around the wall, to see what might be on the other side, and found a small fruit-tree growing there, in the shadow of the stone. From one branch of the fruit-tree hung a royal crown, as if its owner no longer had use for it, and had carelessly left it there.

On the same branch perched two white birds. As soon as the birds saw Randal, they lifted themselves into the air with a rustle of wings, and flew off together toward the south, leaving the crown on the branch behind them.

"Who do you belong to?" Randal whispered. "I can't leave you here where anyone can come along and steal you."

He lifted the crown from the branch. It felt heavy in his hands, and he tried to put it back where he had found it. But when he did so, the branch dipped under the weight of the golden circlet, and the crown would have fallen onto the dirt if he hadn't caught it in time. It seemed to grow even heavier as he stood holding it.

I can't put it back, Randal realized. *I touched it, and now I'm responsible for it. When will I learn that I shouldn't touch what I don't want or don't understand?*

The crown was dragging him downward, pulling him down onto his knees with its ever-increasing weight. *If I can't let go of it, I'll never be able to stand up under the burden,* he thought. *But it won't go back where I found it—what do I do now?*

Then the answer came to him, not in a flash of insight, but more as if it were something he had always known. *I have to put the crown on the head of the true ruler . . . then the barren land will be green and living, and the broken walls made whole.*

In that same instant came the booming of the great bell over the field, and Randal awoke. He lay for a while, feeling oddly restless. The images from his dream still haunted him, filling him with a sense of important things waiting to be accomplished. *But what have I to do with crowns and kingdoms? In dreams, the answer always seems so clear, but when I wake . . .*

After lying still for a little longer, he rose and went to the open flap of the tent to look out at the night.

The stars had traveled a long way across the sky, and the camp was silent. The whole plain full of tents was quiet and dark—the moon had already set. Then, a little way off, a horse nickered.

Let's see what's going on over there, Randal thought. He called up a ball of cold-flame, the magic light that wizards used in place of candles or lanterns. What it showed almost made him cry out and lose the light entirely.

Men were converging on the center of the camp—armed men, with their swords drawn, and all of them wearing the yellow surcoats of Lord Fess.

Randal quenched the blue-white ball of light, but one of the men had already turned toward him. Even with the light gone, Randal saw the man raise his sword.

Randal had trained as a squire before he studied wizardry, and now he used the reflexes gained in his early years to drop and roll away from the blow. At the same time, he called a flash of blinding light and a boom of thunder, loud enough to wake Walter and half the camp besides. Then he rolled back to his feet, making ready a shock-spell as he rose.

The man who had tried to kill him was ducking into Walter's tent. Randal threw his shock-spell. The magic hit the man like a heavy fist, doubling him over and knocking him down.

"Walter!" Randal shouted. "Lys! Wake up!"

Walter ran out of the tent, his broadsword in his hand and his shield on his arm.

"What is it, Randy?" he called out. "Give us light so we can see!"

The young wizard cast the light-spell again. This time, he poured far more power into that simple conjuration, and a huge ball of white fire appeared over the center of the baron's army, lighting the ground all around with a glare like the sun seen through clouds. The whole plain was illuminated in harsh white highlights and dark black shadows.

Walter set the men-at-arms under his command in a circle around the tent that held Vespian's paymaster and the chests of gold. Then, from out of the darkness, a voice cried, "Sir Walter—over here! We need you!"

Walter hesitated, looking over at Randal.

"It's all right," Randal said, "I'll hold things here."

Walter sprinted out of the circle of spears and in the direction of the heaviest fighting. Randal watched his cousin go, and then turned back to holding the light-spell as long as he could, standing motionless while shouts and the sound of clashing steel rose up from other parts of the field.

Overhead, the sky toward the east went from black to gray, and the noise of battle faded to a few scattered outcries in the distance. At last, as the great bell once more gave out its low, brazen note, Randal let the magic fade. The light went from blue-white to dull red and then winked out. He sat down, exhausted, on the ground.

In the dawn light, Sir Walter entered the defensive circle and strode up to Randal. The knight's face was grim. "Well, cousin," he said as he sheathed his sword, "welcome to the war."

II.

Hunting

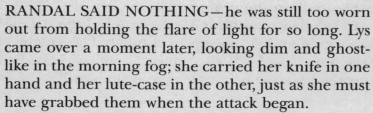

RANDAL SAID NOTHING—he was still too worn out from holding the flare of light for so long. Lys came over a moment later, looking dim and ghost-like in the morning fog; she carried her knife in one hand and her lute-case in the other, just as she must have grabbed them when the attack began.

"What was all that about?" she asked.

"A sortie from the castle," Walter told her.

The lute player frowned. "A what?"

"A surprise attack," Randal said tiredly. "They must have come through Bell Castle's postern gate—that's a castle's smallest gate, and the best hidden—trying to wear down our spirits and test our strength. And now, after that light I cast, they have to know there's a wizard in the camp."

Walter didn't disagree. "It can't be helped," he said. "If you hadn't given us the warning, things might have been a lot worse. It was a nasty business, just the same—we found our scouts and sentries dead with their throats cut. Here—" He flipped something small and metallic through the air to Randal. "What do you make of this? One of the attackers was wearing it."

Randal caught the object, and turned it over on the palm of his hand for closer examination. He saw a little piece of bronze on a loop of red string—not much to look at, but his skin prickled at the magical power clinging to the scrap of metal. He looked again, and saw that someone had scratched a design into the bronze.

Randal looked up at his cousin. "I'm not sure . . . the markings aren't exactly the same as the ones I know . . . but I think this is a sleep rune. It would explain how Fess's soldiers got into the center of the baron's camp: It's easy to cut the throat of a drowsing sentry."

He clenched his fist over the medallion, so tightly that the long scar that ran across his right palm ached with the pressure. "I learned the sleep rune as a means of bringing rest and peace to a person in need of healing—but whoever made this amulet intended it for harm."

"So there's a wizard inside the castle," said Walter.

Randal nodded. "I'm almost certain."

"Then like it or not, you're part of the siege," said Walter. "And you'll be wanted at the baron's council of war."

Walter's prediction turned out to be correct.

15

Later that same morning, Randal sat with his cousin in Baron Ector's pavilion—the largest one on the field, big enough to hold a table and several camp-chairs. Besides Randal and Walter, all of the baron's household knights were present, including Sir Guillaume. The leader of the mercenaries was there as well, a small, wiry man with yellow hair fading to dull gray.

"I won't deny that our task is a difficult one," said Baron Ector, when they had all taken their places. "Bell Castle's garrison is small, no more than twenty men-at-arms, and Lord Fess doesn't rule here in person—he's put one of his knights in charge as castellan, to hold the castle for him—but the walls are high and the castle is well-supplied with food and water. And Fess himself is the strongest lord in all the central region. If he brings all his might to the relief of Bell Castle, we'll be crushed between the hammer and the anvil."

He glanced at Randal, and then turned to Walter. "Can your cousin give us some protection from spies and eavesdroppers?"

Randal had begun to grow weary of the baron's habit of talking to him through Walter—*as if I didn't speak the same language as the rest of them,* he thought—but he held his peace. He was already the odd man out at the baron's council, being younger than all the others and the only one not wearing a sword; he couldn't see any point in starting a quarrel by standing on his dignity.

Walter looked at him with a raised eyebrow. "Randal?"

"I can do it," he said.

Walter turned back to the baron. Randal didn't wait to listen to his cousin relay the answer; he was already pondering which spell would be best for his purpose. A magic circle would hide the tent completely—but after holding the flare for so long during the night attack, he didn't want to use that much energy.

Besides, he reflected, there was no need for such a showy display, when a variant of the basic illusion-spell would serve as well. A few words, a few quick gestures, and the spell was in place, covering the words of the discussion with a blur of noise that would provide a listener with whatever he expected to hear. Only another wizard would be able to tell that the tent was protected. Randal leaned back in his folding camp-chair and listened to the discussion going on.

"Brecelande needs a High King," the baron was saying. "Nobody here disagrees with that. And Lord Fess has a ward, Lady Blanche, who stands to inherit a good part of the kingdom—she's the daughter of the old king's cousin and, as the last surviving member of the royal family, the only one with any legitimate claim to the throne. The lady was betrothed to me in her cradle, before the old king died and his daughter vanished—but now Fess has broken the marriage agreement. He's gone looking to arrange a match with Duke Thibault, one that will bring more power into his own hands. For that reason, good sirs, I am determined to take Bell Castle and bring out Lady Blanche."

Walter stirred restlessly in his seat. "Does this mean we'll be seeing you as High King, my lord?"

The baron frowned at him. "Better me than no one at all," the war-leader answered. "And better me than some painted puppet with Lord Fess pulling his strings."

A brief silence followed the baron's words. Then a grizzled older knight shook his head and said, "Bell Castle's strong—we'll never take it by assault."

"We won't need to," the baron said. "The kindom's had three bad harvests in a row; even Bell Castle is going to be short of supplies. If we can keep the siege going all through the coming harvest . . . well, starvation has brought down stronger fortresses than this."

The grizzled knight looked unconvinced. "As you say, the harvests have been bad. If we neglect our own crops, we'll *all* starve this winter, and what good is a High King then?"

"None at all," the baron admitted. "That's why I've hired Captain Dreikart and his mercenaries to keep the siege going while we send our own men back to their lands for the harvest."

The grizzled knight gave Dreikart a suspicious glance and said to Baron Ector, "Surely you aren't going to trust this business to a band of foreign hirelings?"

The baron shook his head. "They'll be loyal enough—all they have to do is sit on their hands and draw their pay until my own sworn men return." He paused and looked over at Walter. "Besides, Sir

Walter here has brought a wizard along with him. If our enemies have magical help, he'll be able to counter it."

Randal felt the eyes of the assembled knights turn in his direction. Their expressions varied from doubtful to downright hostile, and he was aware that he had few—if any—friends among that group.

Just Walter, he thought, *and maybe Sir Guillaume. The rest of them are following the baron's lead, and he doesn't seem to care for wizards very much. Not that it's going to stop him from expecting marvels. . . . I don't suppose it would do much good to tell him again that I'm only a journeyman.*

The pause stretched into a long silence. Randal realized that the baron was waiting for him to say something. "I'll do what I can, my lord," he said finally. "The first step will be to find out what sort of wizard Lord Fess's castellan has at his command . . . master or journeyman, Schola-trained or self-taught, strong or weak."

"Can you do that?"

At least he's speaking to me instead of talking through Walter, Randal thought. Aloud, he said, "There are spells for such things."

"When will you be able to give us an answer?"

"Tonight when the camp is quiet," Randal promised, "I'll work the magic and see what I can find."

The council continued, but Randal found his interest lagging. The baron was right that only a siege could bring down Bell Castle—taking it by storm would mean dragging scaling ladders and battering rams up the steep slope to the gates of the fortress, with men dying every step of the way. But not even necessity could make a siege interesting.

Baron Ector's army sits outside the castle walls, Randal summarized wearily, *and Fess's men sit inside them. And either the food in the castle runs out before Lord Fess comes to break the siege, or it doesn't.*

If the food did run out, Randal hoped that Fess's castellan would ask for terms of surrender, rather than trying to hold out to the end. By tradition, any castle taken by storm was fair game for looting and pillage; and after the horrors of an assault, the baron's men would want more than gold and silver—they'd want revenge, blood in return for blood.

The council wore on, but nothing else of importance was decided. At length Baron Ector nodded to Randal. "You can end your spell-workings now, wizard—we're done."

The rest of the day was taken up with the bustle and confusion of striking camp, as the greater part of Baron Ector's men left the field and Dreikart's mercenaries took their place. Night had fallen by the time all of those who were going had left, and the moon was just rising. The great bell tolled a single deep, vibrant note, as it had every hour since Randal had first heard its voice. The sound, and the sense of magic that came with it, reminded him of his promise to the baron.

Time to look for wizards, he thought. He found a quiet corner of the camp and made ready to cast the spell of magical resonance, the spell that would bring back a kind of magical echo from any enchanted object or source of magical power in the near distance.

The spell cast successfully. Randal sent the magic forth, and in a moment the echoes of power returned. Not surprisingly, the night air was thick with magic. The sleep rune now resting in his pouch gave off an echo; and so did the castle bell. Beyond that, someone in the castle was indeed a wizard, with the particular flavor of a Schola graduate—*there's something familiar about that presence; I feel as if I ought to know it somehow*—but even stronger was the echo Randal got from another wizard outside the castle walls.

Power. Great power, but no training . . . not from the Schola, at any rate. I wonder if that's the one who made the sleep rune. Randal cast the spell again, and then shook his head. *I don't think so. This power doesn't have that kind of twist to it. But as for whether the magician is a friend or an enemy—I can't tell unless I talk to him.*

Randal allowed the spell of resonance to lapse, and drew his journeyman's robe more tightly around his shoulders. He wondered briefly if he should tell his cousin where he was going, or what he was going to do.

No, he decided. *Walter would insist on coming along— and so would Lys. I can handle this alone.*

Then he stopped and shook his head. *A wizard shouldn't lie, even to himself. I don't know if I'll be safe or not . . . that second magical echo was too strong for a hedge-wizard or a village healwife. I just don't want my friends to suffer because I'm about to go looking for trouble.*

Randal headed back toward the center of the

baron's camp, where Walter and his troop kept watch over the gold. The field seemed different— quieter, with less confusion and disorder—now that most of the knights and their men-at-arms had gone and only the baron and the free company remained. The sound of Lys's lute playing came to him on the night air. He followed the sound, and found her sitting by a campfire, with a group of soldiers nearby listening as she sang.

> "There is a castle in the north
> Built of iron and stone,
> And none within that castle's walls
> But a lady guards it alone."

Lys looked up as Randal came into the circle of yellow firelight. He sat down on the ground beside her and waited for her to finish the song. When she was done, she waved away her audience's requests for more and turned to look at him.

"Hello, Randy," she said. "You've been off by yourself for quite a while. What's going on?"

"I was looking for wizards," he said. "Somebody made that sleep rune, after all . . . and not so long ago, either. The scratches on the metal were fairly fresh, not worn down like they'd be on some amulet that had been passed from hand to hand for a long time."

"And did you find anybody?"

Randal nodded. "I did. There's a Schola wizard inside the castle—I think that's where the sleep rune came from, because their echoes have something of the same feel—and then there's somebody else outside the walls."

"Another of your Schola wizards?" Lys asked.

"No," said Randal. "That's why I came by here—to tell you I have to leave camp for a bit. I want to find whoever it is, and see for myself what kind of wizard can have the magical reserves of a Schola-trained Master of the Art, but not be one."

The lute player gave him a worried look. "Is that safe?"

"As safe as dealing with a strange wizard can ever be."

"Not very," said Lys. She was silent for a moment while her hands picked out a tune on the strings of her lute. "I don't suppose you want company in case of trouble."

"Not this time. Wizards can be unpredictable—"

The corners of Lys's mouth quirked upward. "I'd never have noticed."

Randal ignored the jest. "As I was saying, unpredictable, and not all of them like strangers. Two people might be in more danger than one. If I'm not back before the castle bell strikes twice more, tell Walter where I've gone and decide for yourself what to do next."

He stood up before she could voice more objections, and strode out of the camp. None of the sentries stopped him to question his going out of the camp after dark—his dark, hooded journeyman's robe was the same color as the night, and it took only a minor illusion-spell to direct a watcher's at-

23

tention elsewhere at crucial moments. With the tents and campfires behind him, Randal entered the woods, heading in the direction of the unfamiliar magical echo.

A long while later, he came to a narrow footpath. It led in the direction he wanted to go, so he followed it. Soon he heard the sound of running water. He came around a large boulder into a patch of open ground, and stopped.

Ahead of him, blocking the path, a stream flowed like a ribbon of liquid silver in the moonlight. The fast-moving water frothed up into pale lacework over dark rocks rising out of the current, then plunged over a little waterfall and dissolved into a dim blue mist.

A wooden bridge—no more than a couple of rough-hewn planks—crossed the stream just below the waterfall. On the far bank stood a stone cottage with a thatched roof, the sort of place a free peasant or a prosperous villager might call home.

But there's no plowed field beside it, thought Randal, *or other cottages. Only the woods . . . and the power.* For he knew by the feel of it in the air, as heavy as the scent of sage and savory that came to him from the cottage's herb garden, that he'd found the source of the unfamiliar magic.

III.

The House in the Woods

RANDAL PAUSED FOR a moment on the bank of
the stream. Here, on this side, he was as safe as anyone could ever be in the midst of a countryside at
war. But the stream marked the boundary of the
strange wizard's territory, as plainly as the edge of
a magic circle or the locked door of a secret workroom. On the opposite bank, he would be within the
other's power, and getting out again might not be
as easy as crossing over.

Gathering his courage around him like a cloak,
Randal stepped onto the bridge and crossed the
stream. He walked up to the cottage, and saw that
the windows were unshuttered, and the door stood
open. The inside of the cottage looked dark and
empty. Cautiously, he circled the building, and
found nothing but the herb garden and a few rows
of vegetables.

Before he'd even completed his circuit of the cottage, Randal felt sure he was being watched. At the same time, he was convinced that he was the only human creature in the little clearing. But a wizard, he reflected, might employ many kinds of guardians. When he reached the front door again, he rapped with his knuckles on the wooden doorjamb, but got—as he'd expected—no answer.

He made ready a shielding spell, in case of need, and looked through the open door. There was no light inside the cottage except what little moonlight filtered in from the clearing, but he could make out a single room, with a fireplace at one end and a sleeping loft at the other. No furniture, except for a single table and chair—whoever lived in the cottage didn't get many visitors.

Still, Randal found himself unable to shake the feeling of being watched. The young wizard retreated to the edge of the clearing, and sat down on a stone to wait.

He wasn't sure how long he sat there; the soft, herb-scented night air made him sleepy and uncertain about the passage of time. After a while, an owl came circling down into the clearing from the sky above the cottage, and settled on the sill of the window nearest him.

Randal tried to move, but his arms and legs felt heavy and boneless, like sacks of grain. *Magic!* his mind clamored; he tried to break away, but he wasn't able to. He couldn't touch the strange spell. It twisted away and grew stronger every time he tried to seize hold of it, until soon his entire body had gone numb, and he sat there, helpless.

The owl was a large one, and dark-feathered. It turned its head toward him, and looked directly into his eyes. Randal's arms and legs abruptly regained feeling. Then the bird flew up from the sill and into the dark interior of the cottage. A moment later, the warm yellow glow of candlelight shone out into the clearing.

A woman appeared in the open doorway. She had long, reddish-brown hair—*the color of an owl's wing,* thought Randal—and wore an overdress of brown wool covering an underdress of creamy linen. At first glance he thought she was young, no older than his cousin Walter at the most. Then the light shifted, and he saw her fleetingly as wrinkled and careworn but somehow ageless.

She looked at Randal for a moment, and then said, "Won't you come in?"

Randal got carefully to his feet. He still felt slow and tired in the aftermath of the spell, and suspected that if he tried to run, or even to move suddenly, the woman would have only to fix him with her penetrating, wide-eyed gaze and he would be as helpless as before.

"Who are you?" he managed to say.

"One who means no harm," she told him. "But you are bold to come to my home, and demand my name before naming yourself."

"I'm Randal of Doun," he said. Then, in the Old Tongue—the language of conjuration, and the com-

mon speech of wizards everywhere—he added, *"I left the Schola nearly two years ago."*

But the woman only looked puzzled, as though he spoke in the language of an unfamiliar country. *She doesn't understand,* Randal thought. *Whatever she is, she's not a Schola wizard.*

"My name is Danna," said the woman, after a moment's pause. "And since you've come this far, let me make you welcome."

Randal followed her into the cottage. Inside, the candle-glow bathed everything in warm yellow light, but he couldn't see any candles burning, or any fire on the hearth. A loaf of new-made bread lay in a wooden dish on the table. Although the fire had been cold and the table empty only a short while before, the smell of baking filled the air.

Danna pointed to the single chair. "Sit and eat," she said, and when he hesitated she laughed. "This isn't Elfland, young Randal—the food here is safe enough."

Randal paused a second longer, then sat down in the chair and broke off a chunk from the still-warm loaf. The bread tasted sweet and chewy in his mouth, not like the stale travel-rations he'd lived on since leaving Peda. Across from him, Danna seated herself on a second chair that he hadn't noticed earlier—and then he looked again, and saw that she sat on nothing but the empty air.

Randal's skin prickled. *If she's using a regular levitation-spell, I should have sensed it working. This is powerful magic indeed, and there's nothing of the Schola in it.* He

29

set the crust of the bread down on the table with a shiver.

If Danna saw his reaction, she didn't show it. She sat and looked at him, and then said, "You're the one who cast the bright light last night."

"Yes," said Randal. There was no point in denying it; to a wizard of Danna's power, his own magical touch would be plain in anything he did. He countered with a blunt statement of his own. "We were set upon by attackers bearing a sleep rune. Was that your doing?"

"You already know that it was not," said Danna. "Do you have the medallion with you now?"

He reached into the pocket of his robe and pulled out the piece of bronze on its red cord. "Here."

Danna took it from him, and held it balanced for a moment in her palm. "This belongs to the castle-wizard. And once something has been turned to harm, it's best destroyed."

As Randal watched, she closed her hand over the metal disk. A warm breeze blew through the open door and ruffled Randal's hair. Then the red cord dangling from Danna's fist vanished; when she uncurled her fingers again, the amulet was gone.

"There," she said, like a housewife who had just swept down a particularly large and ugly cobweb. She wiped her hands together, and then looked at him straight on. "Now tell me, young Randal: You're a wizard, and sworn not to use weapons of steel. Why have you come here with those who bring destruction to this land?"

Randal looked down at his hands—one clean and

unmarked, and the other marred by its ugly scar. The last time he'd picked up a sword to defend himself, the blade had cut him to the bone. "I have no desire to carry out destruction," he said slowly, not looking up to meet Danna's eyes. "The war was here before my coming. Now I stay here to help my friends in the baron's army, and to keep a promise I made in another country."

"I know you didn't start this war," said Danna. She stood, swinging herself down from her perch on empty air, and came around the table to stand over Randal where he sat. "But you have power, young Randal—you can stop it, if you will."

Randal shook his head. "I learned magic for the love of the Art, and not to make other people's lives worse by meddling in them. The first wizard I ever met told me that a true wizard has no business looking for worldly power, and everything I've seen so far has proved him right."

"Do you think so?" asked Danna. "Then come with me."

She turned and walked out the door, not looking to see if Randal followed. He waited a moment longer, then rose to his feet and went after her. She had already crossed over the narrow footbridge, and Randal quickened his own pace to catch up with her on the other side. Together they went down the forest path, with Danna leading the way.

The path twisted and turned through the woods, taking Randal and Danna farther and farther back into the hills. Once again, he grew uncertain of the passage of time—had they been walking for hours on end, or for only a few minutes? Then the path ended abruptly in a clearing edged with crude shelters made out of brush and fallen wood. Men, women, and children, all of them ragged and thin-featured, huddled together around tiny campfires.

"You see," Danna said. "Here are the people who lived in the village below the castle, who plowed the fields where your army is camped. When winter comes, these are the ones who will freeze for lack of shelter, and starve for lack of grain."

"Why aren't they inside the castle?" Randal asked. "There, they'd at least have shelter, and food while it lasted."

"Lord Fess has told them time and again that he'll feed no extra mouths in times of siege or famine," said Danna. "Do you blame them for not staying to ask Fess's castellan if their overlord spoke the truth?"

Randal shook his head, and stood looking at the clearing for a long time. He knew for himself what life could be like on the bottom rungs of Brecelande's ladder. As a journeyman wizard, he had no fixed place in the world, and only his own powers stood between him and just such a cold and hungry winter.

And there had been a time when he couldn't even claim that protection . . . when the Regents of the Schola had forbidden him to use magic, and then had sent him out into Brecelande alone and on foot to find the only wizard who could lift their ban. *There wasn't a day in all those months when I wasn't hungry,* he remembered. *I worked for table scraps—and I was grateful even for those.*

Nor had the hunger been the worst of it. He could still remember what it felt like when the lords of the land decided to take out their bad humor on somebody who didn't dare fight back: the angry voices in the dark of the inn yard—"Churl! Do you dare turn your back on a knight!"—the careless backhanded slap that had left his cheekbone cut and bleeding, the heavy boots that had kicked him when he fell.

The memories pressed thick around him, and he shivered. *If Walter hadn't chanced along and pulled me out of that one, I might be dead now.*

Walter hadn't even recognized his cousin, but had stepped in to rescue an unknown stableboy. *He'd help these people, too, if he could*, thought Randal. He turned toward Danna. "You say I have power. What would you have me do with it?"

Her answer came back promptly. "End the siege."

"Your strength is greater than mine," said Randal. "I can see that plainly enough. Why not sweep Baron Ector's army from the field, and end the siege yourself?"

"I may yet be forced to do so," Danna told him. "But that would give Lord Fess the victory . . . and Fess is no friend of mine, or of my people here."

"Then why not see to his defeat?"

"Because I *am* Fess's enemy," she said. "The bell knows it, and the spells worked into the bronze when it was cast will not let me cross the castle walls."

33

"Then neither could I cross them," said Randal. "Lord Fess is no friend of mine either."

"Your power may be able to go where mine cannot," said Danna. "If you wish to help me and my people, then I will help you in return. If not, then stay with your dream of magic for magic's sake alone . . . and I will do what I must to end the siege myself, regardless of the cost."

As she spoke, Randal heard the great bell tolling again from the castle. He blinked, and saw that once more he stood at the outer edge of the forest, looking across at the baron's army. Danna was nowhere in sight.

Deep in thought, Randal started across the open ground toward the sentry lines. When he drew nearer, he could see that the camp was full of unusual activity—voices raised in anger and accusation, and groups of men milling about by shifting torchlight.

Something's happened while I've been gone, thought Randal. He'd scarcely formed the thought before two knights on horseback rode out past the sentries and thundered up to him.

"You—wizard!" one of them demanded. "Where have you been?"

The man's tone offended Randal. "About my own business," he said shortly, and kept on walking toward the camp.

"And what would that business have been?" the other man asked. Randal heard the steely whisper of a sword coming out of its sheath. "You come with us."

Randal looked at the knight who had spoken. *It wouldn't take much effort to break away,* he thought. *They aren't carrying any protection against magic. A flash of light would panic the horses, and I'd be gone before they could find me.*

But running now would leave Walter and Lys to face the trouble—whatever it was—alone, and wouldn't solve the problem of Danna and her people.

And who knows how far Danna's power really extends? Randal wondered. *She's more than just a self-taught wizard, I'm certain of it. Back at the Schola, the masters spoke of beings who live in a place and guard that land and its people. If she's one of those, and goes against the power of the bell to break the siege herself—if that happens, she could unleash enough magical energy to make storming the castle look like a child's game. Nobody within ten miles will be safe.*

He sighed. *I have to stay . . . and besides, if I run I'll never find out what's going on.*

"I'm at your disposal," Randal said to the knights.

Without further word, the two men wheeled their horses around and fell in on either side of the young wizard. Thus, flanked by armed and armored guards, Randal came to the baron's tent. The two knights dismounted and escorted him inside. Then they bowed and withdrew, and Randal was left standing in front of the baron.

In contrast to the magical yellow glow that had filled Danna's cottage, the atmosphere within the tent was dark and murky. A pierced tin candle-lantern hung from the center pole, swinging a little in the night breezes and sending oddly shaped patches of shadow dancing across everyone inside. By its light, Randal saw the baron, sitting in the same chair he'd used at the council of war that morning; to one side of the baron stood Walter and Lys, and on the other, Captain Dreikart.

Randal looked over at Walter. What he saw didn't cheer him—his cousin was pale and tight-lipped, as though he'd shut his mouth hard on angry words before they could be spoken. Beside the knight, Lys stood clenching and unclenching her fists, her blue eyes furious.

And Captain Dreikart . . . Randal let his gaze travel onward to the captain of mercenaries. Dreikart had lost none of his composure, but he was not smiling.

Randal bowed to Baron Ector. "What is it you want from me, my lord?"

The baron scowled at him. "What have you done with the gold?"

Randal blinked. He hadn't been certain what to expect—a demand for some kind of magic, perhaps—and the sudden question took him by surprise. "The gold?" he asked blankly. "Nothing, my lord."

"Where were you, then, these two hours past?"

Talking with a very powerful self-taught wizard . . . or something . . . who's thinking seriously about using magic to sweep this whole field clean. Aloud, Randal said only, "I don't understand. Has something happened to the gold?"

"Somebody," said Walter—the words coming out

36

with sharp edges, as though cut off with a knife—
"*somebody* entered the tent where the chests were
kept, stabbed the paymaster near to death, and took
all the gold away."

IV.
Blood and Gold

RANDAL FELT AS though the ground were slipping out from under him. *Does Walter believe I did it?* Then he realized that Walter's anger was directed at the accusation, not at him, and the world steadied again. He turned back to the baron. "Are you accusing me of theft, my lord?"

"You're the only person who wasn't accounted for inside the camp," said Baron Ector. "I ask you again—where were you, and what were you doing?"

"I was in the woods," Randal told him. "Looking for wizards, as I promised."

"A likely story," said the baron. "That stolen gold was wizard's work—no one else could have carried the chests away without being seen. So far, you're the only wizard we've got."

Randal drew a deep breath. *I can't lie—but it won't help Danna and her people if I tell Baron Ector about her.*

I'll have to tell as little of the truth as I can, and as much as the baron will believe.

"Lord Fess has a wizard working inside the castle," he said, after a moment's thought. "I don't know what rank he is. The sleep rune that brought down our sentries was his doing."

Captain Dreikart spoke for the first time. "The wizard is right, lord Baron. We know that your enemies had a sleep rune; I myself saw the charm when Sir Walter took it from the prisoner who wore it."

"We've been here for weeks, and not a hint of wizardry," said Baron Ector. "This boy arrives, and the same night there comes a magical attack with a sleep charm. That is too much of a coincidence. And where is the charm now?" he asked, his gaze fixed upon Randal. "Tell me that, wizard."

Randal didn't like the way the questions were turning—but he was a wizard, and if he spoke anything other than the truth, his magic would become twisted and unreliable. Once again, he chose his words with care. "The medallion has been destroyed, my lord."

Baron Ector snorted. "So you say. But I think you wore the sleep rune yourself when you slipped past the guards and stabbed Prince Vespian's paymaster in the back. Then you used your magic to remove the gold to wherever you've hidden it, and now you're counting on the same magic to get you out of here."

Randal could only shake his head mutely at the baron's statements. *He knows so little about wizards.*

Lys's angry voice rushed in to fill the gap. "Randal

39

would never do a thing like that!" she insisted. "He's a wizard—and everybody knows that wizards can't use steel. As for taking all that gold, he wouldn't take a crust of bread if he was starving to death!"

Baron Ector raised his graying eyebrows. "So now a vagabond lute player is asking me to believe the oath of a traveling wizard?" he asked. "Fine words, from as masterless a pair of creatures as ever walked the earth."

Randal drew a sharp breath. Before he could speak, Walter took a pace forward.

"My lord Baron," the young knight said in a level tone, "I have already said I would vouch for my cousin with my life. If you won't take his word, then you're calling me a liar as well—and any man who calls me a liar, I can no longer serve."

"Walter," Randal protested, "there's no need—"

Walter barely looked at him. "Be quiet, cousin. My lord Baron has made this a matter of my own honor, as well as yours."

The baron's features, already set in suspicious lines, had darkened as Walter spoke; and the young knight himself, Randal saw with despair, was wearing his stubbornest expression. *Once Walter gets like that there's no bending him—and Baron Ector's not the sort to let open defiance go unpunished.*

Very quietly, Randal began to make ready the magic he'd been unwilling to use only a few minutes before. *If worse comes to worst,* he decided, *I'll let Walter handle the baron and save the shock-spell for Dreikart.*

But the hired captain apparently had ideas of his

40

own. He broke the angry silence with a sharp, "Enough! My lord Baron—young sir—we solve nothing by this. Let me ask the wizard a question." He looked at Randal. "Answer for yourself this time. Did you have anything to do with the theft of the gold?"

Randal shook his head. "Nothing."

"Then that's an end to it," said the captain to the baron. "In my country, too, we have wizards . . . and we know that they cannot speak lies and keep their magic for long."

There was a long silence. *The baron needs Dreikart and his troops,* Randal thought. *But does he want Bell Castle enough to listen to him?*

Finally, Baron Ector made an abrupt gesture with one hand. "Go, then," he said to Dreikart, "and take these three with you if you believe them. But don't let me see them again."

"Very good, lord Baron," said the mercenary captain, with a short and none too respectful bow. He looked toward Randal. "Come, wizard—and your friends with you."

Dreikart turned and walked out of the tent. Randal followed, with Lys and Walter close behind. As they went down the hill Randal saw the dark shape of an owl ghosting across the night sky. *Danna,* he thought, *keeping watch to see what I do next. As if I didn't have enough problems.*

Captain Dreikart broke the silence. Without looking at Randal or breaking stride, he said, "I hear that you can cure men with your magic."

"I know some of the spells," Randal answered.

"Then follow me and heal this paymaster. When he is well again, he can tell us where the gold has gone."

Without further word, Dreikart led the way to the tent where the chests of gold had been kept. Inside, by the dim light of a second candle-lantern, Randal saw Prince Vespian's paymaster lying face down and unmoving on a straw pallet. One of Dreikart's men sat on a low stool nearby; he looked up as the captain ducked under the tent flap, and said something in an unfamiliar tongue.

Dreikart nodded, and turned to Randal. "He does not wake, Gisli says. Do what you can, and we will see if your magic works for you or not."

Randal wasn't surprised. "A test, Captain Dreikart?"

"You could say that, yes," Dreikart replied. "If your spells fail you, then maybe you lied back there. But if you heal him, then it's likely you were telling the truth."

Walter spoke for the first time since defying the baron. "So, you'd make the life of one man into a rope to hang another?"

Dreikart shrugged. "Why not? The paymaster loses nothing—without a wizard, he dies anyway."

"He's right, Walter," said Randal. The young wizard had already knelt beside the pallet and had pulled back the blanket. Somebody—Gisli, perhaps—had bandaged the wound in strips of clean linen, but blood had soaked through the white cloth in a large red splotch low on the man's back. Randal pointed to the bloodstain. "That's a death-wound, and you know it."

Walter fell silent. Randal looked from his cousin to Lys, and then over to Dreikart. "I'm not a master wizard," he told the captain. "Just a journeyman. I may not know the right spells. Even if my spells work, they may not be strong enough to heal a wound like this. If they fail . . . whatever you do, let Sir Walter and the lute player go."

Dreikart shook his head. "I will promise nothing. Do your magic, then we'll see what happens."

Randal sighed. It didn't take wizardry to see that arguing with Dreikart would do no good. "As you will," he said quietly, and turned away from the captain to touch first the paymaster's ash-pale forehead, and then the side of his neck. Under Randal's fingers, the man's skin felt cold and clammy, and the pulse in the great artery was fast and weak.

"*Dormi,*" Randal murmured in the Old Tongue, invoking the spell of rest and comfort. He had to take off the bandage next, and for that, a sleep-spell was kinder—and easier for the healer as well.

Carefully, he peeled away the bloodstained linen and laid it aside. Just below the paymaster's ribs and next to the spine, the knife wound gaped open like a deep, red-edged mouth. A trickle of blood ran out across the dead white of the paymaster's skin in a crimson line.

Randal concentrated on working the spell to stop the bleeding and close the wound. Soon enough, it was done, and he sat back with a tired but satisfied sigh.

Then, without warning, the paymaster's pulse once again grew weak, and his breathing shallow. Beads of sweat broke out all over the man's skin. Randal leaned forward again, and reached out a second time with his magical senses. This time, he found what the man's injury had masked earlier: Even before the dagger had pierced his flesh, the merchant had been struck down by another wizard's spell of sickness.

Randal bit his lip. *I don't dare use one of the spells that break all others . . . right now, magic is the only thing holding this man together. I'll have to break this spell, and this one alone.*

He examined the spell as closely as he could, trusting to his magical senses. The magic had a traditional feel to it: It was the sort of thing that could be learned at the Schola, not like what Danna had done in the forest. Randal knew, at least in theory, how to break such a spell—although even for someone who had the skill, the process was one of trial and error, rather like picking a lock.

His head fell forward on his chest, and his own breathing grew slow and deep as he searched within himself for the hidden keys to the spell of sickness. Bit by bit, as he found them, the spell weakened and fell away from its victim.

At last, the paymaster sank into a healing sleep, and Randal stood. His head whirled from breaking the sickness-spell, and he leaned against the tent pole until the dizziness had passed. Lys thrust a cup of water into his hands, and he drank greedily.

"Thanks," he said when he had finished. He

turned to Dreikart. "Now are you satisfied that my word is good?"

Dreikart nodded. "You are a true wizard, yes. Now we will wait. When the paymaster wakes, we will ask him what he remembers."

Randal sat back against a wooden box, and listened, half-sleeping himself, as Lys began again to sing to the melody of her lute. The tunes were cheerful at first, but a darker thread soon appeared.

"Johnny ate of the venison
And his dogs drank of the blood,
And they all fell asleep in the good greenwood,
Asleep as they'd been dead, dead,
Asleep as they'd been dead."

Outside the tent, the sky grayed on toward dawn. At last, the paymaster's eyelids twitched open, and he awoke. He tried to stand, but his legs wouldn't support him. Randal and Walter caught him before he could fall, and eased him back down onto the pallet.

"Lie still," Randal said. "You've been hurt. Can you tell us what happened?"

"Hurt?"

"Stabbed. The gold stolen. Who did it?"

"I—I don't know. I don't remember. I was walking into the tent, and then the next thing I knew I woke up here with all of you around me."

"I don't like this," Dreikart said to the paymaster. "I had hoped that my questions would be answered, but what you've said makes the mystery deeper."

45

"It's worse even than you think," Randal said. "The other wizard, the one in the castle, had a hand in this—I know the feel of his work by now. If you want to know where the money is, look up in Bell Castle."

"What if the gold is not in the castle?" said Dreikart. "Then my men sit through your baron's siege for him, and maybe take the castle, too, all for half pay. And that is not what we agreed to, you understand."

"Your agreement isn't—" Walter began.

"Leave it be," said Randal tiredly. He felt wrung out from the long healing spell, but it looked like he would be doing magic again before the morning was much older. He turned to Dreikart. "No one is going to sneak those six chests out through the baron's army—if the gold was taken into the castle, it'll still be there when the castle falls. But if you want to be certain, I can use magic to see what happened and where the gold went."

The young wizard glanced over at the paymaster. "I don't dare use that fellow as a focus, though," Randal said. "He's still healing—making him into the center of a major spell would kill him for sure. I'll have to find somebody else who was close to what happened."

Walter was already shaking his head. "Nobody besides him went near the gold all evening. My own men stood guard all around the tent—I could see the entrance myself from the campfire where Lys was singing."

"That's close enough," said Randal. "It'll make

my work a bit harder, maybe, but not impossible." With the heel of his boot, he drew a circle in the packed earth of the tent floor, just missing the straw pallet where the paymaster lay. "Lys, Walter—stand with me inside the circle. And Walter, leave your sword outside the circle."

"I don't like that," Walter said.

"Captain Dreikart can hold it," Randal explained. "If you carry it, the spell may not work."

Walter handed over his sword, and Lys dropped her eating knife. The two stepped into the circle, and Randal bent down to mark the signs of the four directions, murmuring in the Old Tongue as he worked. Then he inscribed the words and symbols of the spell of looking backward, and the crudely drawn boundary blazed into glowing blue life.

"Now we've begun," said Randal. "The circle is closed, and no one can leave until I break it open again."

"Look at the light outside," Lys said. "It's changing."

They all turned toward the open tent flap, and Randal heard Walter mutter something under his breath. Within the circle, nothing had altered: The shadows remained where they had lain when Randal cast the spell, and a cool morning breeze still fanned the hair of everyone inside the circle. But darkness filled the tent outside, and the paymaster slept unwounded on his straw pallet beside the chests of gold.

"We're looking at things as they were last night," Randal said. "Now all we can do is wait and watch."

"Can anyone else see us?" Walter asked.

"In our true time, yes," said Randal. "Anyone who looks will see us in the circle. But they won't be able to enter."

"Something's happening," said Lys.

The lute player spoke the truth. A small, glowing spot had appeared on the ground inside the tent. It flowed upward and lengthened into a slender column of golden light.

"I didn't see anything like this last night," Walter said.

"You weren't inside the circle then," said Randal. "Someone is opening a magic portal. At my guess, the other side of the door is somewhere within the castle."

As they watched, the glowing column grew into a cylinder about a yard across and three yards high. A man in chain mail stepped out of the cylinder. He wore a closed helm that hid his features, but something about his movements seemed tantalizingly familiar.

As Randal and the others watched, the man drew the knife at his belt, then bent over the sleeping paymaster and stabbed him in the back.

"So *that's* what happened," Walter said. He sounded puzzled. "But the tent was guarded the whole time, and I was there within earshot. Why didn't I see any of it?"

"Look outside," said Randal, pointing to the tent flap. A pale line of blue fire ran past the tent's opening. "Another magic circle. The wizard in the castle cast it to hide everything that's going on, including

48

the circle itself. If you'd been inside the tent, you'd probably have been magicked to sleep and then stabbed, just like our friend there."

More men came out of the pillar of golden light as Randal spoke. They began passing the chests of gold back into the portal. Just as the last chest was being loaded, one of the men looked up, and saw Randal.

That's impossible, Randal thought. *We aren't really here. He* can't *see us!*

Nevertheless, the man's eyes were locked on Randal. The man called something into the pillar, and pointed at the three who stood inside of their own circle.

Randal felt a sudden wrench as magic surged out from the pillar of gold. The light flared up like a bonfire—bright, blinding. Randal covered his eyes with his forearm against the painful brilliance. Then, abruptly, the light ceased.

He lowered his arm, and saw darkness. Glowing green afterimages floated in the air in front of him, no matter where he looked, even on the inside of his closed eyes. The afterimages faded, but the light didn't return.

Am I blind?

"That was a good trick, Randy," Walter's voice came to him. "Now will you please tell me where we are?"

"You mean you don't know?" came a voice from the dark. "You're in the dungeons of Bell Castle."

V.
The Wizard of Bell Castle

SOMEWHERE IN THE darkness, Walter said, "Are you sure taking us here was a good idea, Randy?"

From closer by, Lys's voice replied, "He probably had his reasons."

Randal ignored both of them. He could take care of their imprisonment later: Locked doors and dungeon walls didn't present much of an obstacle to a practicing wizard, not even to a journeyman who hadn't yet taken the examinations for mastery.

Meanwhile, the problem of how they had landed here nagged at him. It was none of his doing, he was sure of that. And the other voice, the one that had first spoken, had stirred up an old memory in the back of his mind, something unpleasant that had to do with darkness and pain. More than anything else, right now, he wanted to get a good look at the speaker.

He called up the cold-flame to see the features of their fellow prisoner—but no blue light came at his call. Only a blank, empty feeling, as though he'd reached out to touch something dear and familiar, and found an impenetrable wall in its place.

He tried again for the cold-flame, but still nothing happened. His magic was shut away where he couldn't reach it, on the other side of that blank wall. *So close,* he thought, with a muffled groan, *and so useless.*

"Randy?" came a whisper from close by. He felt the warm touch of Lys's hand on his shoulder. "Is something wrong? Are you hurt?"

He shook his head. "Not hurt—no," he said, trying to keep the confusion and worry out of his voice.

"Then what's wrong?"

She's known me for too long, Randal thought. He drew a deep breath. "My magic," he said. "Something is blocking it."

As he spoke he heard a single deep, distant note— the stroke of the great bell, muffled by the massive stone walls of the castle.

"That's what's doing it, you know," said the voice that had first spoken. "The bell. Only the castle's own wizard can work magic inside the walls, as long as that bell tolls once every hour."

Randal turned his head toward the speaker. Now that the dazzle of the portal's golden brilliance had faded, the darkness around him had grown slowly less complete. He could make out the grille of a cell door at one side of the room, where faint grayish light came from a window somewhere out of sight.

It wasn't the clear, stark illumination of a cold-flame, but enough light penetrated the gloom to reveal a man sitting half-propped against the dungeon wall.

Although the prisoner's face was turned toward the newcomers, all Randal could make out of his features was a pale cheek and what might have been an arrogant, high-bridged nose. The rest was hidden by the man's thick blond hair, falling forward across his face. But still the feeling of familiarity nagged at Randal. The young wizard stepped away from Lys's reassuring hand, and went over to kneel beside the prisoner, where the light from outside shone most directly.

This close, Randal could see that the prisoner had been ill-used. Bruises mottled his fair skin, and blood from a split lip had caked on his mouth and jaw. What further damage was hidden by the man's tunic—fine linen under the grime and blood—Randal couldn't begin to guess.

"Who are you?" he asked.

"Three days ago," said the prisoner, "I was the castellan here. But now the wizard holds the castle himself, and I'll be hanging from the battlements tomorrow morning."

Walter came to stand at Randal's shoulder. The two cousins looked at their cellmate.

"I know your voice," said Walter, after a while. "Since we are prisoners together, even if only for a little while, we should trust one another with our names." He paused. The man on the floor made no answer, and Walter went on. "I am Sir Walter of Doun."

The man gave a faint chuckle. "Then introductions aren't necessary," he said. "We've met before. I'm Sir Reginald de Haut Desert."

Randal drew back a little.

Now I remember, he thought. *I remember the bruises you and your friends gave me, when I was sworn not to use my magic, and you thought I was just a stableboy . . . and I remember what happened later.*

Later, the tournament of Tattinham had ended with Walter lying face down in his own blood, hit from behind with a mace that had crushed his shoulder. Walter hadn't seen the one who brought him down, but rumor had blamed Sir Reginald for the dishonorable blow.

If Randal remembered, so did the others. Even in the dark of the cell, he saw his cousin Walter stiffen. "I know you well," Walter said. "If it should be our good fortune to escape this cell alive, we have business with one another."

The prisoner lifted his head slightly, with some of the pride that Randal remembered from their first meeting. "I give you my word—the blow that struck you down at Tattinham was none of my doing."

"So you say." Lys's voice, coming from farther back in the cell, was cold. "But why should we believe you?"

Sir Reginald extended a hand in her direction— Randal watched it lift, and then fall back to the straw when Lys made no move to come forward. "I pray

54

you, Demoiselle, be kind. I die tomorrow; why should I tell you lies today?"

Next to Randal, Walter still had not relaxed. "Anyone who'd strike down a man from behind would probably keep on lying in the teeth of death itself . . . but tell me who you say struck the blow."

Sir Reginald laughed, a faint, painful sound. *He's hurt worse than he looks,* Randal realized. *Bruises all over, and maybe a broken rib or two—enough to make a few careless blows in a dark inn yard look tame by comparison.*

"Better to ask that question of your allies in the baron's camp," said Sir Reginald. "Sir Guillaume of Hernefeld has more gold than he should. And he knows full well that I never struck that blow, because he did it himself."

"And went about Tattinham putting the blame on you?" Randal had found his own voice again at last. "That's a strong accusation to make."

"But a true one," said Sir Reginald. "If you ever see your own camp again, ask friend Guillaume how he paid Duke Thibault the ransom for his horse and armor, when he himself owned nothing more than that on the day of the journey."

"Thibault. . . ." murmured Walter. "The duke owed me ransom himself that day, after I captured him during the mock battle."

"Owed it," said Sir Reginald. "But never paid it. When the time arrived for claiming ransoms, you lay wounded; 'dying,' many said."

Lys stepped forward out of the shadows, and dropped down to sit beside Randal on the straw-covered floor. She looked across at Sir Reginald, her expression halfway between skepticism and belief. "You're claiming that Duke Thibault let Guillaume off paying his own ransom, in return for agreeing to kill Walter?"

"Yes."

Lys's expression didn't change. "The duke has more gold than any of us will ever see. What's the price of a horse and armor to a great lord like him?"

Again Randal heard Sir Reginald's painful laugh. "A duke's ransom is more than that of some tourney knight. Sometimes towns or castles have been the ransom demanded and paid for lords of his rank. You would have been a rich man, Sir Walter, at the Duke's expense—and he's as proud as he is wealthy."

"An interesting story," said Randal. "If it's true." He looked directly at Sir Reginald. "You told us that the wizard here displaced you as castellan. Why?"

Sir Reginald's chin came up. "He claimed I was disloyal—although I swore to keep Bell Castle safe from siege and assault, and never broke that oath."

"Then what *did* you do?" asked Lys, at the same time as Randal asked, "Where did this wizard get the authority to displace Lord Fess's appointed castellan?"

"I've done nothing for which I need to feel ashamed," said Sir Reginald. "But the wizard thought differently, and he is Lord Fess's own nephew."

"Ah," said Lys. "That explains a little."

"But not enough," Walter cut in. "You never paid

me your ransom from that tourney, either—I'm claiming it now. An explanation will clear the debt nicely, I think."

But Sir Reginald shook his head. "I'm sorry. The explanation isn't entirely mine to give, not without—"

"It doesn't matter," said Randal quietly, as much to his cousin as to Sir Reginald. "Not right now. Someone's coming."

A light was bobbing closer along the passage outside the cell. It came nearer, and Randal saw that it was a lamp, carried by a young woman dressed in elegant clothing. After the near darkness of their prison, Randal found the small flame glaringly bright.

At the sight of the woman, Sir Reginald struggled to rise to his feet.

The lady ran forward. "No—don't!" she cried out, going down onto her knees outside the cell. Light and shadow danced crazily on the walls as she set the bronze lamp down on the floor beside her and reached out to touch Sir Reginald's fingers through the grille.

"The wizard keeps a close watch on me," she whispered rapidly. "I couldn't come here any sooner."

"My lady, you shouldn't have come here at all," said Sir Reginald. "It will only make him angrier if he finds us together."

The lady was shaking her head. "There's nothing he could do to me that is worse than keeping us apart. I couldn't let you sit here all alone."

Sir Reginald gave her a painful smile. "You are kindness itself," he said, with a formality that Randal guessed must cover an inward struggle for self-control, "but I already have companions."

The young woman looked over toward Randal and the others, though without letting go her grip on Sir Reginald's hands as she turned. In the yellow lamplight, Randal could see that she was fair-haired and blue-eyed, but not especially beautiful—rather plain, in fact, with a narrow face and a long, thin nose gone pink at the tip from weeping too much in private. But her eyes, in spite of their red rims, were kind and intelligent.

"Who are you?" the lady asked. "And how did you come here? I've never seen you before, and no one's opened the gates. . . . I've been watching."

Walter bowed, as courteously as if a cell door had not separated him from the lady. "We're from Baron Ector's camp outside the walls," he said. "Walter of Doun, my cousin Randal, and Demoiselle Lys. It appears this wizard of yours set a trap and we fell into it."

"There is nothing he likes more than puzzles and snares," the lady said in a bitter tone. She looked around at the dark stone walls and iron bars. "He toyed with us, he watched and waited, and thanks to that boy wizard and his everlasting traps we are come to this."

Randal looked over at the young woman. "I think I'm starting to understand things now. Are you the Lady Blanche that Fess is trying to marry off to Duke Thibault?"

"I am," she said bitterly. "And whom he promised before that to Baron Ector of Wirrell, and would promise again tomorrow to somebody else, if he thought that a new match would bring him more power than the old one."

"But until tomorrow morning," said Sir Reginald, "she is above all the Lady Blanche who is my wife."

There was a startled noise from Walter. "Your wife . . . but how?"

"There's a wise-woman in the woods nearby," said Lady Blanche, "who's witnessed the handfastings of the village-folk for more years than anyone can remember. We left the castle in secret, by the postern gate, and went to her."

It must have been Danna, Randal thought, but said nothing.

Lady Blanche shuddered a little. "The wizard was waiting for us when we returned."

"And he did this to you?" Walter asked Sir Reginald.

The castellan nodded, wincing a little at the movement. "He was . . . not pleased."

Lys was shaking her head slowly in the shadowed darkness. "If the wizard is Lord Fess's nephew," she said, "and shares his uncle's ambitions, then I'm not surprised he wants to hang you from the battlements. A wife isn't so easily married off, but a widow is another matter altogether."

"You distress my lady," said Sir Reginald sharply.

But Lady Blanche had paid no heed to the lute player's remark. Instead, she was looking closely through the grille at Randal, with hope beginning to lighten her features.

"You wear the hooded robe," she said to him. "Could it be that you also are a wizard?"

"Only a journeyman," Randal answered. "But it doesn't matter. As long as the castle bell keeps ringing once every hour, my magic is useless inside these walls. If you could only destroy the bell somehow—"

"Strong men have tried to break that bell," protested Sir Reginald, "and never dented the metal. How can a young woman succeed where they failed?" Sir Reginald clasped the Lady Blanche's slender hands tightly through the grille. "My lady, don't anger the wizard further on my account, or he might forget his fear of his uncle, and do you some harm."

Blanche smiled at Sir Reginald, and then looked back at Randal. "He's right," she said. "Alone, I could never destroy the bell—but what if I can keep it from ringing at the appointed time? What then?"

Randal felt the first stirring of renewed hope. "I can't be sure," he said. "But there might be a chance."

"Then I'll do my best to stop the bell from ringing," said Blanche. "After that, you'll have to escape as best you can—only take my husband with you when you go."

"But what about you?" cried Sir Reginald. "What will become of you?"

"Don't worry," said Blanche. "As long as Lord Fess wants to play kingmaker in Brecelande, he'll treat me as his greatest treasure. And while you live he can never marry me to Duke Thibault or any other—so in your safety lies freedom for us both, and if we're patient, perhaps happiness someday as well."

She untwined her fingers from Sir Reginald's, and picked up the bronze lamp. "Be ready, all of you," she said, rising to her feet as she spoke. "I don't know how long this may take."

Her footsteps and the glow of the lamp faded away down the corridor. Sir Reginald knelt, leaning against the grille where their hands had clasped, and said nothing. The others waited in uneasy silence.

Finally, Walter spoke. "Someone else is coming—not the lady."

Randal listened. Soon he, too, heard soft, padding footsteps drawing closer to the cell, and a hooded figure came into view outside the grille. Unlike Lady Blanche, the newcomer scorned to carry a lamp; instead, he paused outside the cell door, and lifted a hand.

A blue-white tongue of cold-flame appeared, and made hard-edged black shadows on the walls of the cell. Randal blinked in the sudden glare, and looked up from where he knelt beside Sir Reginald.

He saw a young man—a boy, really, scarcely older than himself—dressed in the black, hooded robe of a journeyman wizard. But unlike Randal's travel-stained garment of plain cloth, the newcomer's robe was cut from rich black velvet, with sable fur lining the hood and the long, full sleeves. A bronze medallion on a leather cord hung around his neck.

So this is the wizard Blanche and Sir Reginald are so afraid of, thought Randal. *Maybe he's not as dangerous as they make out. He's certainly no master.*

Then the other wizard pushed back his hood, and all Randal's new-formed hopes vanished. He knew those features only too well—he'd seen them every day during his years at the Schola, and the passage of time hadn't changed them all that much. The sallow cheeks were a little plumper, the black hair a little sleeker, but the expression in the heavy-lidded brown eyes—a peculiar mixture of smugness and discontent—was still the same.

The wizard of Bell Castle, and Lord Fess's nephew, was unmistakably Gaimar, Randal's old roommate at the School of Wizardry: Gaimar, who had laughed at Randal's first clumsy attempts to master the art of magic; Gaimar, whose malice had driven Randal out of his room in the dormitory and into lodgings in the town; Gaimar, who had always been a better wizard than Randal, even in their apprentice days.

I suppose I shouldn't be surprised to find him in charge of Bell Castle, Randal thought. *Back at the Schola, everyone said that he was related to some great lord or other.*

In the blue light of the cold-flame, Gaimar looked at Randal and smiled. "Of all the people I never expected to catch in my little trap . . . and wearing a journeyman's robe, at that. I wonder if the Regents of the Schola know you're wearing it? The last I heard, they'd thrown you out."

"That was a long time ago," said Randal. "A lot's happened since then." *If Gaimar doesn't know for certain that I've passed my apprenticeship,* he thought, *then I don't need to tell him. His ignorance may be my only advantage.*

Gaimar smiled. "But you haven't changed much that I can see. Still second-rate—you can't have had the skill to set off my trap unaided."

Randal tried to seem as ignorant as Gaimar thought him. "Trap?" he asked. "What trap?"

Gaimar looked pleased with himself. "When someone broke up our surprise attack," he said, "I knew Baron Ector had brought a wizard with him. But I had agents and plans of my own—I arranged to have the baron's gold stolen, in a way that only a wizard could accomplish, because I knew that the first thing a competent wizard would do to clear his name was cast a spell of looking backward. The rest was just a matter of adjusting my magic circle, so that anybody using magic to watch from the future would set the trap in motion and be transported here. But you never had the kind of power it takes to work spells like that—who helped you?"

Randal shook his head. "Who do you think it might have been?"

"Come, come," said Gaimar. "Don't try to play games with me. You should know better. And don't try to lie: Sooner or later, lies will twist the little bit of magic you might have learned by now, and then where will you be? Out of luck, that's where."

"Nobody helped me."

"You expect me to believe that?" sneered Randal's old roommate. "You couldn't even light a candle until you were halfway through your second year at the Schola, and you barely squeaked through your examinations. Which of these others was it, now?"

He stared hard at each of the prisoners in turn—first at Walter, dismissing him with a quick shake of the head. "Not you . . . musclebound oafs of your sort ought to know better than to oppose me." His gaze moved on to Lys. "That leaves you, as I suspected all along."

Gaimar smiled at Randal. "I suppose I owe you my thanks. I've been trying to catch that shape-shifting hedge-witch ever since she dared help this disloyal lout of a castellan run off and marry the Lady Blanche. But she kept slipping away—if you hadn't attached yourself to her and drawn her into my trap with you, she'd still be free right now."

He thinks Lys is Danna, Randal realized. *The bell's protection must be hiding the fact that she doesn't have any magical energy to speak of.*

Lys, meanwhile, didn't miss her cue. "The contest between us isn't over yet," she told Gaimar. "I'm willing to wait."

Gaimar laughed. "Then wait—and see where your patience takes you. Tomorrow's dawn will find all three of you hanging from the battlements beside Sir Reginald." He laughed again, extinguished his wizard light, and walked off.

After he had gone, the prisoners sat in the darkness, too dejected for speech. Far above them, the

64

bell tolled another hour, and Randal shivered at its note.

How many more times will the bell ring before tomorrow's dawn? he wondered. *Everything depends now on the Lady Blanche. If she can't reach the bell and silence it, then we haven't got a chance.*

VI.

The Tower

TIME PASSED SLOWLY in the dungeon. Randal sat on the straw-covered floor between Lys and Sir Reginald, watching the faint light in the passage outside change as the day wore on. Walter paced back and forth from one side of the cell to the other. Nobody seemed inclined toward conversation. And every hour, the great bell tolled.

Randal sighed, and dropped his forehead onto his upraised knees. *It's no use,* he thought. *There's no way Lady Blanche can get to the bell . . . not with Gaimar and a whole castle full of men-at-arms in her way. We're all going to die tomorrow morning, and there's nothing I can do about it.*

Lys must have heard the sigh. Softly, she began to sing another one of the old ballads of Brecelande.

"Fly down, fly down, my bonny bird,
And light upon my knee.
Your cage shall be of beaten gold
and your perch of ivory."

Randal sat listening to Lys's clear alto voice, and let himself forget, for a while, about the fate that would meet him and his friends when morning came. Then, just as Lys was beginning the song's last verse, Randal felt something change—Bell Castle's weight no longer seemed to press down on him as heavily as it had a moment before.

He lifted his head.

Nobody else in the cell seemed to have noticed the change. Quietly, still not daring to hope, Randal held out one hand and summoned the cold-flame.

For the space of a heartbeat, the magic did not answer. Then, a pale blue radiance blossomed above his hand like an opening flower, filling the whole cell with light.

Randal didn't hesitate. He stepped to the cell door, laid his hand on it, and spoke the unlocking spell. No magic fastened the door: Gaimar had been so confident in the power of the bell that he was relying on iron alone to hold a wizard captive. Randal heard the bolt turn within the lock. Walter saw what Randal was doing, and put his shoulder to the grille as his cousin stepped back. The door swung open.

"Your lady was as good as her word," Randal said to Sir Reginald. "She's managed to silence the bell."

"Then we must make haste," said Sir Reginald. He pulled himself to his feet and stood hanging onto the iron grille for support. "She's put herself in danger to save us—we have to find her before the wizard does."

"No," Randal said. "She told us to get you out of Gaimar's reach. Show us the way to the castle's postern gate, and once you're outside the walls, I'll do what I can to help her."

Sir Reginald let go of the grille with one hand, and pointed down the passage. "The postern gate is that way," he said. "Run if you must. I will not leave my wife behind."

Randal felt his temper beginning to rise. "What good will it do anyone," he asked, "if you make her a widow a few hours sooner? And don't talk to me about running—if Gaimar tries to stop us, I'm the one who has to stand and fight him."

"Forget it, Randy," Walter said. He slipped a shoulder under Reginald's arm. "I'm with Sir Reginald. When I was knighted, I swore an oath to aid the helpless, and all those in distress. I don't see that I have a choice."

Randal recognized his cousin's inflexible tone. *Trust Walter to do what he thinks is right, regardless of the consequences.* Nevertheless, the young wizard made one last, desperate attempt at reason.

"How are you going to rescue anyone?" he demanded of Sir Reginald, who stood clinging to the iron grille. "You can barely stand."

Walter glanced over at Randal. "Randy, can you heal him?"

Randal sighed. "I can," he said. "But it'll put him to sleep for a couple of hours. Once we're outside the castle—"

"No," said Sir Reginald.

"There must be something you can do," said Walter. "You healed the paymaster, and his wound was a mortal one."

"Just because a thing is simple doesn't mean it's easy," Randal told his cousin. He turned to Sir Reginald. The castellan was looking worse than ever in the blue glow of the young wizard's witchlight. "I can help you a little," Randal told him. "There are spells that can block pain, and lend you strength for a little while. But it's not a true healing. The help it gives is only temporary, and when it wears off, you'll still be hurt—probably worse than before."

"If Gaimar has his way," said Sir Reginald, "then tomorrow I'll be dead. Do what you can, and quickly."

Randal laid his hands on the castellan's shoulders, closed his eyes, and focused on the transfer of magical energy that formed the core of the spell. He could feel himself weakening as the energy flowed from him to Sir Reginald, but he knew that his reserves of power were deep enough to make up for the loss.

Life's odd, he thought as the spell ended. *That night near Tattinham, all I could think of was how much I wanted to hurt Sir Reginald. And now I'm weakening myself to keep him alive.*

As the spell ended, Sir Reginald straightened and

stood unsupported. "That's done," he said. "Let's find my wife and be gone."

"It may not be that easy," said Walter. "We still have the castle garrison to get past—but if we open the main gate and let Captain Dreikart's troop in, the confusion should be enough to cover our escape."

Sir Reginald shook his head. "I won't see my wife put in any more danger, even to escape. Your Baron Ector would not use her any more kindly than her guardian has done."

"Leave Baron Ector to me," said Walter. "I give you my word—while I live, I'll see that no one presses your lady into doing anything against her will."

There was a brief silence. Then Sir Reginald nodded slowly. "We'll need weapons," he said, pointing to the right. "The armory is this way—we'll arm ourselves, and then I'll go to the bell tower while you strike out for the main gate."

"Wait," said Randal. The two knights turned and looked at him. "I'd better be the one to bring back Lady Blanche," he said. "Opening the gates may draw off the castle's men-at-arms, but Gaimar will be trying to save the bell before anything else. Anyone hoping to reach Lady Blanche is going to have to fight him—and I'm the only one of us who knows how."

Sir Reginald gazed at him with mixed hope and reluctance. "Bring my wife out safely, wizard, and I'll be forever in your debt. But are you sure you can do it?"

"Nothing is sure," said Randal, "except that it won't be a matter for swords." He turned to Lys. "Are you staying with Walter?"

She shook her head. "I'm with you. Let's go."

The knights were partway down the corridor in the direction of the armory before she finished speaking. Randal set out half-running after them, with Lys following close behind.

At the end of the passage, a flight of stone stairs led upward. Randal and Lys took the steps two at a time, and emerged into the open air. Afternoon sunlight surrounded them, achingly bright after the dimness of the cell below. From somewhere up ahead came a slow, regular booming sound.

Then, before Randal could go any farther, a wave of dizziness passed over him, coming out of nowhere and forcing him to lean against the stone wall for support. At the same time, he felt an overwhelming awareness of powerful magic, much like his reaction to first hearing the sound of the great bell—and coupled with that the mental snap that told him of a spell going into effect.

"What happened?" asked Lys. "What's wrong?"

"I don't know," said Randal, straightening. "But there's some kind of magic at work here—not the bell, but something new—and I just felt it take hold."

"We can't let it stop us," said Lys.

"We won't," said Randal. "Come on."

They ran on, going up more steps and under a stone archway. In the shadow of the arch, they

71

halted, and looked out across an open space at the source of the booming noise.

A dozen men-at-arms in the yellow surcoats of the castle garrison stood outside the door of one of the castle towers. The men carried a heavy wooden beam between them, and were pounding it against the thick, iron-banded oaken door. They didn't have much room to swing it in—the castle's builders must have deliberately placed the tower in a cramped corner of the castle yard, to frustrate enemies who might try to batter down the door.

"That's the bell tower," said Randal. "Lady Blanche must have shut herself inside."

"But how are we going to get to her?" asked Lys. "Can you take on so many at once?"

"I don't want to," said Randal. "Anything I could do to stop so many would probably kill all of them, and that's not what I want to do."

"Then how—?"

"There's another tower nearly as tall as the bell tower," Randal said. "If we can get up there, then I can show Gaimar a trick or two."

He looked about the courtyard. A knight in armor shouted orders at the laboring men, the castle dogs barked and howled at every muffled boom of the ram, and servants craned their necks around the edges of doorways to watch the commotion.

Walter and Sir Reginald probably haven't left the armory yet, Randal thought. *Lys and I still have a little time.*

"There," he said, pointing toward another door on the far side of the courtyard, beyond the bell tower. "That should be the entrance to the great hall. We can get to the tower from there while everybody's watching the ram."

Lys wet her lips. "No disguises?"

"We shouldn't need them," said Randal. "And the longer I hold off working any more magic, the better—why should I make it easy for Gaimar to find us? Let's go."

They strolled across the courtyard casually, as if they belonged there, past the laboring men-at-arms and through the open door. As Randal had predicted, the door led into the great hall of Bell Castle. The long, high-ceilinged room, with bright yellow banners hanging from the crossbeams and swords and shields lining the walls, reminded him of his old home at Castle Doun. At the far end of the hall, a fire blazed in an open hearth—and Gaimar stood silhouetted against the flames.

Randal halted on the threshold. Gaimar laughed out loud, the mocking sound echoing off the vaulted ceiling. "You escaped from the cell," he called out, "but what good has it done you? Any half-trained apprentice can open a lock. You still have to deal with me—with me, and with the power of the bell."

Randal swallowed, trying to find words for a reply. Before he could speak, Lys's clear alto voice rang out beside him.

"Do you really think so?" the singer demanded. "How long is it since the bell struck last?"

Gaimar sneered. "You know the prophecies, I see—but do you know all of them? While the bell is whole, this castle shall never fall—and no member

73

of the house of Fess shall ever die inside these walls."

Lys put her hands on her hips and laughed at him. "Then I'm surprised you ever had the courage to step outside them."

She's buying me time, thought Randal, as he looked about the hall for a doorway that might lead up to the second tower. He saw only one, an archway just to the right of the hearth where Gaimar stood. Calling his power to him, he prepared the spell of visual illusion. He cast the spell, and a fighting man with a drawn sword ran in through a door on the other side of the hall and charged at Gaimar.

Gaimar didn't flinch. "You'll have to do better than that, you know," he said, as the fighter swung his blade. The illusory steel passed through Gaimar's body without leaving a mark behind. Then the phantom vanished, and the wizard of Bell Castle smiled.

"Why not try some reality?" he asked, and spoke a word of power. At his command, the weapons hanging in the great hall tore loose from the walls and arrayed themselves in the air. Another word, and the swords and axes and spears began to advance on Randal and Lys as if carried by invisible hands.

"Randy . . ." breathed Lys.

But before Randal could move, a blast of wind came from nowhere and howled down the chimney into the fireplace. Smoke, flames, and sparks bellied out across the hearth. Little tongues of orange fire licked out and touched the fur trim on Gaimar's velvet robe.

A smell of scorched hair filled the hall, and the floating weapons rattled to the flagstones. Gaimar shouted another word of power, summoning a cold, wet mist to extinguish the flames. While his attention was distracted, Randal grabbed Lys by one arm and ran for the archway he had noticed earlier.

That was a magical wind, he thought as he ran. *But whose? There's no other wizard here except for Gaimar—and Danna, but she can't cross the castle walls.* He decided not to question his luck too much, and kept on running.

Then he heard another shout from Gaimar. "You! How did you get over there?"

Randal looked back over his shoulder, getting ready to defend himself and Lys against a magical attack from behind. But Gaimar wasn't looking at them—he was looking at the archway, his right hand lifted in the magical gesture for breaking a spell.

"Illusions I called you," the other wizard said to something Randal couldn't see. "And illusions you are."

I don't know what he's seeing, thought Randal, *but it gives me an idea.* He halted in his tracks, dragging Lys to a stop with him, and cast the spell of invisibility on them both. *As long as we don't move, and he doesn't think to look for us, we're safe.*

For what seemed like a long time, but could only have been a few seconds, Randal and Lys stood immobile halfway across the great hall. Then Gaimar turned and stalked out of Randal's field of vision.

Randal waited a little longer, allowing time for Gaimar to leave, and then said to Lys, "Let's go."

He ran on through the archway and up the stairs, half-dragging the singer with him.

They reached the top of the tower, emerging from the stairway to stand under the open sky. The sun was low on the horizon. Then Randal heard an exclamation from Lys. Turning, he saw her looking out over the parapet at the tents and banners of Baron Ector's encampment.

She pointed down at the field. "Look," she said.

Randal looked, and saw that beyond the baron's camp an army was advancing to the attack, carrying the banners of Lord Fess and Duke Thibault. So far the baron's army stood firm—Captain Dreikart's mercenaries had formed into ranks bristling with spears that the horses of Fess's riders would not charge—but Ector's men were being pushed back step by step toward the rock spur on which the castle stood.

"Oh, no," Randal said under his breath. "If Lord Fess breaks the siege before we can find Lady Blanche and get out, we're all lost."

And what Fess does to me then, he added to himself, *will probably make Gaimar's plans for Sir Reginald seem merciful.*

Lys pulled at his sleeve. "Come on, Randy. Lady Blanche is over there in the bell tower right now."

Randal looked where Lys pointed, and saw that she was right. Through the high-arched windows of the bell tower, he could see Lady Blanche standing inside the upper chamber, holding a double-bladed axe in both hands—*she must have snatched it from its bracket in the great hall,* he realized, *then run into the bell tower and barred the doors after her.* Now she was laboring, with clumsy strokes, to cut through the great bell's wrist-thick pull-ropes. The blade sliced through the ropes, and they fell away.

He heard Lys cheering beside him. But down below in the castle yard, the men-at-arms swung their makeshift ram against the door of the bell tower one more time. Randal heard a crash, and the sound of splintering wood. The men dropped the heavy beam and pushed through the broken door into the bell tower.

Time to finish the work before they reach the top, he thought, and made ready to summon a bolt of lightning against the bell, to warp its metal and silence its voice forever. But before he could cast the spell, the men-at-arms swarmed into the bell tower. One of them grabbed Lady Blanche and pulled her back down into the stairwell and out of sight. Another man carried a heavy wooden mallet. He swung it back, and then brought it forward to smash against the curved side of the bell.

Once again, the deep bronze voice rang out. The tone was not as rich and full as when the bell's own clapper struck against the curved metal, but the magic was there just the same. Randal felt the lightning-bolt-spell run out of his grip like water, and then his own energy began to ebb as the bell's sound washed over him.

"It's over," he whispered to Lys. "Gaimar's won.

If the bell keeps on ringing, he'll soon have me trapped here, powerless."

But then a flash of lightning came springing up to the bell tower from the castle courtyard below—magical lightning, setting Randal's wizardly senses on edge at the same time as it struck the floor beneath the bell. The man with the mallet danced back out of the way of the flying chips of stone.

That lightning wasn't Gaimar's! he thought. *No more than the wind was. Danna . . . maybe stopping the bell was enough to let her in.*

Randal clung dizzily to the broken stone of the parapet and stared downward over the edge of the tower wall. He tried to pick out the unfamiliar wizard. But if a small woman in a peasant's homespun dress was anywhere about, he couldn't see her—and then the man with the mallet struck the bell again, and the young wizard abandoned all thought for a moment as his power sank even lower. This time, the bell's note brought a wave of physical weakness as well. Randal staggered and leaned against the wall for support.

He looked over at Lys. "I'm stuck here," he said. "But I'm the one Fess and Gaimar are after—if you leave right now, there's a chance they might not look for you."

Lys's blue eyes were wet with tears. She shook her head, but before she could speak, the magical lightning flashed up again from below—weaker this time, as if the unknown wizard down in the courtyard were tiring as well.

That can't be Danna down there, Randal thought. *Nobody with as much power as she has would tire so quickly.*

He straightened. "Whoever that is in the courtyard, he won't be able to hit the bell again," he said. "Not with its sound draining away his power. But the two of us can still give Gaimar a fight before we're done."

He pulled together the remnants of his magical energy, and cast a shock-spell into the other tower, aiming for the man swinging the wooden mallet. The spell struck; the man tottered, and fell out of sight.

Then Randal heard a shout from the stairwell behind him. He turned to see who had come.

Gaimar stood there. "I should have killed you when I had the chance," he said. "This time you won't get away."

VII.
The Bell

"SO YOU SAY, WIZARD."

Randal started at the sound of Lys's voice—only it wasn't Lys who stood beside him now. It was Danna, her russet-colored hair unbound and flying out behind her on the wind that blew from nowhere across the open tower.

Gaimar had halted in his tracks at the sound of Danna's voice. "Accursed hedge-witch," he snarled. "I knew it had to be you."

He lifted his hand, and from the tips of his fingers, a jet of flame shot out at Danna. Randal cried out, and tried to raise a shield-spell to protect her. But Danna made a small, almost invisible gesture with one hand, and the flames dissolved into ragged wisps of white smoke that blew away on the wind.

"Foolish boy," she said. "You yourself have opened the door to your most deadly enemy." She smiled at Gaimar in a way that made Randal's neck prickle. "I have the measure of this place now, and you have both more and less time than you think. Make the most of it—if you can."

Gaimar seemed to crumple at her words, and his sallow skin turned the color of dirty ivory. He raised his hand to his chest and grasped the medallion that lay there. Abruptly, the wizard of Bell Castle vanished.

"Where did he go?" Randal asked Danna.

"To his portal, most likely," the shape-changer told him. "The first lord of Bell Castle paid a mighty wizard of those days to construct a magical gateway between the world outside and the dungeons below the castle. Fess's little wizard has turned the portal to his own uses—such as fleeing from me to work the spell that you felt take effect as we came out of the dungeons. He plays with time, thinking to prevail over us by making what we will do into something that never happened—but he's working with things he doesn't understand."

Randal nodded, struggling to put his whirling thoughts into words. Finally he managed to choke out, "What have you done with Lys?"

Danna smiled at him—a much kinder smile than the one she had given to Gaimar. "No harm, I assure you. She and I only traded places for a while." She pointed upward, and Randal saw a peregrine falcon wheeling and circling against the late afternoon sky. "Now that I must go and set my own work in motion, I can give you back your friend."

Randal caught hold of Danna's wrist before she

could make another magical gesture. "Wait," he said. "Don't bring Lys here into danger."

Danna shook her head with what looked like regret. "I don't have a choice. The bell has only been silenced for a little while, not broken—at this moment, my magic and the spells protecting Bell Castle stand in the most precarious balance. Just as I was only able to enter because Gaimar's trap brought me here, I can only leave if the one whose form I borrowed comes here in my place."

"Then stay here yourself," said Randal. "You have enough power to control Gaimar—why leave all that work to me?"

"The bell weakens me," Danna said. "I can't destroy it, because my own magic is bound to the land which it controls. But you are the outsider, the one not bound—you are the one with power here, not I."

She lifted both arms, and her form seemed to shrink and alter, springing skyward as it changed. A moment more, and a red-brown hawk circled overhead. Another bird-shape arrowed downward as Danna rose—the peregrine falcon, spilling the air from beneath its wings and landing with a flutter on the parapet beside Randal. Shape and color flexed briefly, and it became a black-haired girl in boy's clothing, sitting on the rough stone with her legs dangling.

"Lys!" Randal exclaimed. "When did Danna—?"

The girl swung her feet down to the floor. "Last night," she said. "Somewhere between the baron's tent and the paymaster's, with never a by-your-leave. One moment I was walking along, and the next thing I knew I was roosting on a rock ledge and wondering about field mice for breakfast."

"She shouldn't have done that," said Randal. For some reason, Danna's brief use of Lys angered him in a way that the shape-changer's demands on his own abilities had not.

Lys shrugged. "It wasn't so bad—she let me use her eyes to watch what was going on."

"I still don't like it."

The singer made an impatient gesture. "Let it go, Randy, all right? If I'm not angry, you shouldn't be either. Right now, we need to find Walter and get out of here before Fess's men take the castle."

"It won't be that easy," said Randal. "Walter isn't going to abandon Sir Reginald and Lady Blanche. And there isn't much time."

He ran down the stairs, with Lys following. They reached the archway that led to the great hall, and paused for a moment to look into the big, vaulted room. Once again, Gaimar stood in front of the hearth, his profile toward the stairway entrance, his gaze directed at something outside Randal's range of vision. So far, he hadn't noticed the two watchers in the shadowed archway.

"How do we get past him?" Lys asked under her breath. "From the great hall, he can block the way to both towers and the courtyard as well."

Randal frowned. "Let me think."

Inside the great hall, Gaimar was laughing at something Randal couldn't see. "You escaped from the cell," Randal heard him call out. "But what good has it done you?"

I've heard those words before, Randal realized. *Only minutes ago.*

Now Lys's voice came to him clearly from inside the great hall, speaking as she—or rather, Danna—had spoken when they first confronted Gaimar. "Do you really think so? How long is it since the bell struck last?"

In the shadowed archway, Lys grabbed Randal's arm. "That's my voice in there! Randy, what's going on?"

He shook his head. "I don't know. Something's gone wrong. Time is looping in on itself—that's our own past we're hearing right now." *And if we're still inside Bell Castle when the loop closes,* he wondered, but didn't dare to ask aloud, *what will become of us then? Is this what Danna meant when she spoke of Gaimar having both more and less time than he thought?*

Inside the great hall, Gaimar was still gloating. ". . . No member of the house of Fess shall ever die inside these walls."

And once again, Danna replied in Lys's voice, while the girl herself stood in the archway and gripped Randal's forearm with fingers made painfully strong by fear: "Then I'm surprised you ever had the courage to step outside them."

I know what happens next, thought Randal. *If I look out into the great hall, I'll see myself getting ready to cast the illusion-spell.*

A moment later, a man in armor, with sword held high before him, charged out of the opposite doorway and into the great hall. Just as before, the phantom reached Gaimar and swung an illusory blade. And again, Randal heard Gaimar's mocking voice: "You'll have to do better than that, you know. . . . Why not try some reality?"

Then came the sound of metal clashing against stone as the swords and shields ripped free of their brackets. Randal watched the weapons draw themselves up in battle array and begin their advance toward the threshold of the great hall.

He remembered watching that slow, measured attack, and shivered. Only the wind had saved him then—the sudden chilling draft that had come down the chimney to fill the great hall with smoke. The magician's wind had seemed to come from nowhere . . . *It wasn't Danna after all,* he realized. *It was me.*

"I think I know what I have to do now," said Randal, and called a blast of wind through the chimney.

Smoke and sparks bellied out of the hearth, and the tongues of orange fire reached to the hem of Gaimar's robe. The weapons clattered to the floor as Gaimar's concentration broke. A cloud of gray fog swirled around him, extinguishing the flames that licked at his garments. Still half-shrouded in the thick fog, he turned to look toward the shadowed archway where Randal and Lys stood concealed.

At the sight of them, Gaimar's features contorted with anger. "You!" he demanded. "How did you get there?"

Randal didn't answer. *What could I tell him—"something you haven't done yet has put time into a loop, so that I'm going up into the tower and coming down from it at the same time"? Besides, I didn't hear myself say anything before, so I won't be saying anything now.*

Gaimar made a magical gesture with one hand—Randal recognized the spell for breaking an illusion.

He's trying to dispel us, Randal thought. *He thinks we're unreal.* As Gaimar finished the charm, Randal cast invisibility on himself and Lys. To Gaimar's sight, they would have vanished, just as if the illusion-breaking-spell had worked.

"Illusions I called you," Gaimar said to the archway, "and illusions you are." He turned his back on Lys and Randal, and strode out through the archway on the other side of the great hall.

Randal let out a sigh of relief. "Let's go," he said. "We have to find the others and get out of here."

"But that was—"

"I know," he said. "That's why we have to hurry. With time starting to loop back on itself, we have to get out before the circle closes entirely."

They hurried through the great hall and out into the courtyard. Overhead, the slanting afternoon sun cast long shadows against the stones. The castle's drawbridge still had not fallen. In the courtyard, men no longer labored with the battering ram; instead they were fighting, twelve or more of them, against Walter and Sir Reginald.

The two former prisoners stood together only a few feet away from the heavy wooden lever that would let loose the chain of the drawbridge and open the gates. They'd gotten themselves weapons from the armory—Sir Reginald had armed himself with sword and shield, and Walter had found a two-handed greatsword almost as long as he was tall. Randal was impressed. Not many men had the combination of strength and skill it took to wield a greatsword, but Walter swung the double-edged blade of steel in wicked figure-eight sweeps as if it weighed no more than a willow wand.

None of the men-at-arms appeared eager to come within reach of Walter and the greatsword; in the hands of an expert, the heavy blade could cut through armor. But Sir Reginald, fighting sword-and-shield just outside the greatsword's sweep, looked to be in a bad way. He held his shield awkwardly, favoring the broken ribs that slowed his movements, and as Randal and Lys came out into the courtyard one of the men-at-arms pressed forward and pushed the rim of his shield aside.

The man's own sword came down through the gap the move had created, and Sir Reginald's linen tunic bloomed with the brightness of fresh blood. The sword fell from the castellan's hands. With tremendous effort, he pushed bodily through the line of men-at-arms and seized the lever that freed the drawbridge. He pulled it downward with him as he fell to the ground and lay motionless in a puddle of crimson.

Randal heard the metallic clatter of chain links unwinding, and an echoing slap of wood against stone as Bell Castle's drawbridge slammed open. Then came the sound of hoofbeats drumming on the wooden span, and the high, clear note of a battle-horn. A crowd of horsemen and footsoldiers pressed in through the castle gates, carrying on their helms and spear-points the colors of Captain Dreikart's mercenary company.

Sir Reginald lay unmoving on the ground, with Walter standing over him. *I have to help them,* thought Randal, *and then find Blanche, in the tower or wherever she is by now.* At the thought, he lifted his head and looked upward, narrowing his eyes against the sunlight to see if Lady Blanche—or anyone else—were still visible in the bell tower. He bit his lip: The man with the wooden mallet had returned, and was making ready to strike the bell.

"Not again," Randal said. But the man hit the bell, and the sound, even muffled as it was, struck at Randal like a blow.

Enough, he thought, and lifted his hand. Bolts of lightning had hit the tower at least twice already. Maybe it had been weakened enough that another strike would bring the entire thing down. Gritting his teeth against the weakness brought on by the sound of the bell, Randal cast a bolt at the tower. The lightning struck, and chips of stone flew from the blackened rock.

"It's working!" he shouted at Lys over the racket in the courtyard, and cast the spell again. This time, the bolt blasted free a whole block of stone when it hit, but the force of the spell almost used Randal up. His vision went black for the space of several heartbeats, and his breath rasped in his chest. He sagged back against the wall and waited for the weakness to pass.

"Randy, what is it?" Lys asked.

He shook his head; it was another two long

breaths before he could speak. "I'm tired, that's all. That bell keeps on draining me, and I have to keep going just the same."

"Is there anything I can do?"

"No."

Out in the courtyard, the tumult had grown louder—Randal blinked his eyes clear, and saw that the men riding in no longer carried the banners of Dreikart's company. He saw some men wearing Fess's yellow, and other men that must be Duke Thibault's. The yellowcoats and Thibault's men pushed forward, and Dreikart's men turned to meet them. Knots of fighting men spread across the stone, and up onto the walls; Randal couldn't see Walter any longer.

And the bell is still up there, he thought, *waiting to ring again and drain me dry.*

"I'll try it one more time," he said quietly to Lys. "If it doesn't work, you may have to leave without me."

He stepped forward from the shelter of the doorway, and reached down into the depths of his magical reserves. He built the power, concentrated it, and let it go.

This time the lightning bolt seemed to tear itself loose from the fabric of his own existence—and in the instant the magical energy passed through him, he seemed to feel an echo of its power coming back at him from the far side of the courtyard, almost as if a second, phantom wizard were throwing his own energy into the blow. Then the lightning struck the tower, and stone blasted from the sides, showering

89

down into the courtyard as the men below broke off from fighting to run for cover.

Slowly, and with weighty dignity, the whole top of the tower crumbled and fell—and the great bell tumbled with it, striking the courtyard and shattering into a hundred pieces. The air shivered and vibrated with the sound of its breaking, and then there was nothing in the courtyard but silent bits of metal. The broken edges shone in the afternoon sunlight, and drifts of powdered rock floated above them like smoke in air gone suddenly still.

Then the backlash of the powerful spell struck at Randal with an impact as if he himself had fallen from the tower. The pain and weakness of it shivered all along his body, and he staggered backward.

Lys caught him and lowered him to the ground, supporting him against her shoulder. He tried to tell her to go find Walter and leave before the fighting grew any worse, but his voice refused to obey his will any longer, and the world was starting to fade out around him.

Then, with the last of his vision, Randal saw a large, russet-feathered owl drifting lower and lower, until it came to earth in front of him. The bird changed, until it took the form of a woman. It was Danna.

"Rise now, Randal," she said. "You have done well. But go now. Leave. You have done your work."

She stooped and touched him, and Randal felt new life flow through him. "What about my friends?" he asked.

"You must make your own choice," she answered, "but leaving the castle will be easy for only a short while longer. After that, it may be impossible, even for you."

The woman melted again into an owl, beat her wings, and flew upward into the empty sky.

VIII.
Blood Wedding

SLOWLY, RANDAL GOT to his feet and looked about. Rubble from the fallen tower filled the courtyard, and most of the fighting had gone elsewhere. Randal heard the clanging of weapons inside the great hall, and saw knights and footsoldiers struggling for control of the battlements, but in the yard itself there was a kind of uncertain calm. Beside the gate, Walter stood over Sir Reginald—still watchful, but with no enemies, for the moment, near enough for him to fight.

"Randy!" Walter shouted. "Over here!"

Randal and Lys ran across to the gate. Walter lowered the point of his greatsword to the flagstones. The blade of the sword was almost as long as Walter was tall; when he leaned on it, panting a little after the struggle at the gate, the massive pommel came almost to his chin. He nodded toward Sir Reginald.

"Can you do something for him, Randy? He's in a bad way."

Randal nodded, and knelt beside Sir Reginald on the bloodstained flagstone. He reached out and laid a hand on the castellan's shoulder. Sir Reginald's eyes flickered open at the touch, and his lips moved.

"Wizard?"

"Yes," said Randal. "It's me. Lie still, and I'll do my best to help you."

Sir Reginald shook his head, and caught at Randal's sleeve. "No," he said. "My wife—you promised—"

"Do you want me to tell her I left you lying here dead?" Randal demanded. "Lie still."

I don't dare heal him completely, the young wizard thought. *He'd sleep too deeply, afterward . . . and we still have to fight our way out of here.* He sighed. *Close the wound and stop the bleeding, then, and hope he doesn't hurt himself any worse before today is over.*

A second time, Randal spoke the words that halted the flow of blood from Sir Reginald's wounds, and gave the castellan new energy drawn from Randal's own resources. This time, the sense of being drained lasted longer than before; and Randal seemed to feel each of the injured man's cuts and bruises as his own.

When the spell was done, Randal sat back on his heels, feeling almost as weary as he had after the destruction of the great bell, before he himself had felt Danna's healing touch. Sir Reginald looked even worse than Randal felt. The castellan's face, under the dirt and bruises, was paler than the linen of his tunic—but he pushed himself up to a sitting position and fixed Randal with a bright, feverish gaze.

"My wife, wizard—is she safe?"

Randal looked at the wounded castellan. "Someone as valuable as she is, Sir Reginald, is always safe. But the rest of us aren't so valuable—we should be leaving while the gate is open. Then I can—"

"Are you saying I should leave my wife behind?" Sir Reginald's voice cracked with indignation, and he struggled to his feet. "I thought a kinsman of Sir Walter's would at least be true to his given word—but you're no better than that black-robed pup of Fess's!"

Randal sighed and stood up. "Take my advice and go while the way is still clear," he said. "I'll find Lady Blanche and follow you as soon as I can."

"The others can go," said Sir Reginald. "I'll stay, and see my wife rescued."

"Then we all stay," said Walter firmly. "And leave together with the Lady. Randy, can you find her?"

Randal closed his eyes for a moment. *I wish Sir Reginald weren't so lovesick,* he thought, *and Walter weren't so honorable. Then I wouldn't be risking anybody's life but my own.* Aloud, he said, "I saw Fess's men take her from the bell tower before it fell. With fighting in the courtyard, they'd have had to go through the great hall to reach anywhere else . . . we should look there, first."

"Can you disguise us?" Lys asked. "In case the fighting is still going on in there—or in case Fess's men have won."

Randal nodded. "Stand still a moment, all of

you," he said, and moved his hands in a series of magical gestures. *"Similitudo fallacis,"* he murmured in the Old Tongue. *"Vaga et varia . . . fiat!"*

Randal felt the mental sensation, like a lock sliding into place, that told of a spell successfully completed.

"Don't do anything to draw attention to yourselves," he warned them. "The spell isn't really a disguise—just a weak illusion. Dreikart's men will see us as mercenaries like themselves, and Fess's men will swear they saw us wearing yellow surcoats—but as soon as anybody looks at one of you hard, you'll show up for what you are. In the meantime, though, anyone who sees you will think you belong in the crowd."

"Right," said Walter. "Let's go."

They started across the rock-strewn courtyard toward the great hall. Even before they reached the open doors, Randal knew that they would find time changed again inside. His skin prickled with the awareness of powerful magic at work, of spells being done and undone and tangling Bell Castle in their webs.

But Randal had no chance to pause and cast the spell of magical resonance. He and his companions had already stepped across the threshold of the great hall into a scene of revelry and celebration. Bright banners made patches of color on the stone walls where the swords and axes had once hung, and long tables piled high with food filled the space that had been empty and echoing only a little while before.

95

Or was it such a little while? Randal wondered. *Time here is twisting and uncertain—it seemed I heard fighting in here only a moment ago. How long does it take to clear away the wounded, and scrub the blood away from the stone?*

At the far end of the hall, where Gaimar had stood, the fire blazed even higher than before. In front of the hearth stood two men and a woman. One man wore a yellow surcoat like those of the fighting men who crowded the tables, but his was made of silk and embroidered with borders of gold and silver threads. This, Randal realized, was the great Lord Fess, whose yellow-coated riders had once chased him the length of Brecelande, from Cingestoun to Widsegard. The other man, the one who wore a golden coronet, had to be Duke Thibault. And the woman—

"Blanche!" whispered Sir Reginald.

Unlike her guardian and Duke Thibault, Blanche wore no wedding finery, only the dress she'd had on when she came down into the dungeon. Her yellow hair had come undone, and now hung loose down her back.

They must have brought her straight down from the bell tower, Randal thought, *and kept her guarded ever since.*

Lord Fess turned to face the seated ranks of fighting men who filled the great hall. "Listen, all of you!" he called out in a voice pitched to carry across a battlefield if need be. "I call on all of you to bear witness to the handfasting of Duke Thibault to my ward, Lady Blanche, last surviving member of the royal house of Brecelande. Do you all stand ready

to swear that this wedding has been duly solemnized by declaration before witnesses?"

"Aye!" roared the crowd with one voice.

"No!" cried Lady Blanche before the last of the echoes had died. "Listen to me, everyone—this is a forced match, and I do not consent!"

Fess turned red. "Do you defy me, girl?"

"It's of no importance," Duke Thibault cut in smoothly. "If her guardian swears she consented, and her husband and all the witnesses swear likewise . . . who will listen to a woman who changed her mind after the vows were said?"

"Lying dog!" exclaimed Blanche. "Swear what you like, but I won't marry you—thank Fortune, I'm married already to a man who's worth ten of you!"

"If you mean that fool of a renegade castellan," said Fess brutally, "then you're a widow already. He died in the courtyard, when my horsemen came through the gates."

Blanche went ashy-pale and swayed as if she might faint. Randal, still watching from the threshold of the great hall, heard a voice at his elbow shout out, "Liar!"

"Liar!" Sir Reginald shouted again as he pulled free of Walter's restraining hand. The castellan's half-disguise faded as he strode forward into the firelight. "I live—and I challenge you, Duke Thibault, for pressing my wife into marriage against her will!"

The fool, thought Randal in despair. *He's done for.* He didn't realize he'd spoken the thought aloud until Walter's quiet voice murmured in his ear,

"Maybe—but not many of us could hold our tongues in the face of such an insult. And Duke Thibault will have to answer the challenge, or be shamed in front of everyone here."

Walter seemed to be right about the challenge. A pair of Fess's men-at-arms had seized Sir Reginald as soon as he finished speaking—but Duke Thibault gestured at them to let the castellan go.

"Don't worry," Thibault said to Lord Fess. "I won't let such charges go by unanswered. Since this is my wedding day, however, I prefer to let my champion fight in my place." He turned to the crowded feast-hall. "Sir Guillaume of Hernefeld, come forth!"

And the man who rose from the table nearest Duke Thibault was indeed the young knight who had formerly served with Walter in Baron Ector's camp. Now, however, he wore Thibault's coat of arms, as befitted a duke's champion.

Sir Reginald was right all along, Randal thought. *Sir Guillaume must have been Thibault's man—and Fess's—from the very first, a spy and traitor in Baron Ector's camp. He was the one who struck Walter down at Tattinham, and he was the one who stabbed the paymaster—it was him I saw when I cast the spell to look back in the past.*

Sir Guillaume made a courtly bow to Duke Thibault. "How may I serve you, my lord?"

Thibault nodded toward Sir Reginald, who stood pale and grim-faced between his guards. "This upstart challenges me," the Duke said. "Fight him, in my name."

Guillaume bowed again, without bothering to

look in Sir Reginald's direction. "To the death, my lord?"

"To the death," agreed Thibault. He turned to Lord Fess. "We can push back the tables and settle it now, if you like."

"An excellent idea," said Lord Fess. "Let your champion fetch his armor and make ready." He glared at Lady Blanche. "Once my stubborn young ward sees for herself that this fellow is dead, perhaps she will remember her duty and stop opposing the excellent match I've made for her."

"Not while I have breath in my body," said Blanche. "And this is no fair challenge—my husband comes here with sword and shield alone."

Sir Guillaume smiled easily. "Set your mind at ease, my lady. For honor's sake, I'll forgo my armor in this combat."

It's a cheap promise, Randal thought. *Guillaume's in good health, and he doesn't look like he's seen any hard fighting today—and Reginald's wounds are only patched up, not healed. Just walking around will kill him if he does it long enough.*

The three standing hidden near the entrance watched as the fighting men began pushing back the tables and benches to give the two knights room. Sir Guillaume and Sir Reginald faced each other in the center of the great hall. When Fess called out, "Begin," they began to circle one another, swords at the ready.

Randal laid a hand on Lys's arm. "Everybody is going to be watching the fight," he said quietly. "Now's our only chance to help Lady Blanche and make sure Sir Reginald doesn't throw his life away for nothing. As long as you don't draw attention to yourself, the illusion I'm working will make you fit in with the rest of this mob—can you get to Lady Blanche and bring her out?"

Beside him, Walter stirred restlessly. "You're asking Lys to play the most dangerous part," he said. "Why not one of us?"

"Because I'm an actor and you're not," said Lys. "And Randy's going to be busy working the spells." She turned to Randal. "I'm ready whenever you are."

"Then let's do it now," said Randal.

Out in the center of the feast-hall, the two knights still circled one another. Sir Reginald would be saving his strength, Randal guessed, and Sir Guillaume could afford to bide his time and watch for an opening. The men who looked on were waiting and watching as well—they didn't even glance at Lys as she made her way around the sides of the great hall to where Lady Blanche stood between Lord Fess and Duke Thibault.

I wonder what they'd see if they did look at her? Randal thought. *Another servant, probably—and nobody pays any attention to servants. Sir Reginald never even recognized me as the stableboy he beat up that night.*

Lys was almost at Blanche's side. Randal watched closely, and when he saw her reach out to touch Fess's ward on the shoulder, he cast the two spells he had been preparing. In the next breath, an exact, illusory duplicate of the Lady Blanche stood between the two guards, and Lys and Blanche—both

101

now covered by the vague disguise that Randal had put over the others earlier—began making their way back around the great hall toward the door.

It's a good thing everybody is watching the single combat, thought Randal. *Otherwise we could never have made the switch.*

Then he felt a sudden wrench, as though reality had twisted around him and tried to pull him with it. The strong magic that surrounded the great hall, and all of Bell Castle, had just grown even stronger.

Someone is working a powerful enchantment, he thought. *And this one has a bad feel to it—not like Danna's work. If it keeps up, I'll never be able to hold all the illusions I've got going, let alone think of some way to help Sir Reginald.*

"I'm going to have to go look for Gaimar," he muttered to Walter. "He's putting us all in danger. I can feel it."

"Can you stop him?" asked Walter.

"I don't know," said Randal. "I have to find him first."

He stepped away from the others, working his way around the edges of the room and casting the spell of magical resonance as he moved. *Gaimar is close by. So there must be a magical door somewhere. . . .*

Once he began looking, the door was easy enough to spot—a patch of blank stone that wasn't really there at all. Instead, the illusion hid a deep alcove set into the wall of the castle. Hidden within the alcove was a steep, narrow stairway, leading upward.

Randal paused for a moment, and then began to climb. Every step seemed to take a great effort, not because of any magical opposition but because he was forcing himself closer and closer to a confrontation he dreaded. Memories kept coming back to him as he climbed, images of himself as a first-year apprentice at the School of Wizardry: barely able to read and write in his own language; ignorant of the least syllable of the Old Tongue; possessing nothing but a burning desire to learn wizardry, and unable to unlock the power he knew was hidden within him.

And Gaimar had learned everything without effort, even then—without effort, and without even valuing what he had learned. And now Randal's old schoolmate was pulling together the threads of a spell such as even a master wizard would hesitate to work—for no other reason than that his uncle wanted to play kingmaker in Brecelande.

Court wizard to the power behind the throne, thought Randal as he climbed one more step. *Back at the Schola, the other apprentices always said that Gaimar wanted to be a baron, and his family wouldn't let him. Is this what comes of forcing someone onto a path he doesn't want . . . would I have become like him if I'd had to stay at Castle Doun and train for knighthood instead of wizardry?*

Randal shook his head. He was wasting his time with such thoughts—he needed to find Gaimar before the spell was finished and the trap, whatever it might be, swung shut.

Another step, and he was standing outside a closed door. He stopped, and listened to the sounds coming from within.

On the other side of the door, Gaimar's voice rose and fell in the rhythms of a long and complex spell. Randal frowned, trying to catch the words themselves, and not just their sounds. It was hard to concentrate, with the spell's energies pulling and twisting around him as the words of the chant wove a powerful and subtle structure of magic. The words . . . suddenly the hair rose on the back of Randal's neck.

Gaimar's trying to bring back the bell. To restore it to its former shape, and the castle's protective spells along with it. But the way he's doing it, telling everything to go back to the way it was before . . .

"No!" Randal cried. *"No!"*

He slammed a shock-spell against the locked door, throwing it open. He saw Gaimar's workroom, its walls lined with books bound in glossy new leather, its windows paned with glass. Wax candles in silver holders marked out the four quarters of a magic circle with Gaimar standing at the center, his arms upraised in magical invocation. All around and above the circle, the witchfire glowed, casting unnatural, flickering shadows onto Gaimar's face and hands.

The rising tension of the spell wrenched at the core of Randal's being. Heedless of the danger, he rushed into the workroom, trying only to stop the flawed conjuration before it reached its climax. But he was too late.

"Fiat et finis!" Gaimar shouted triumphantly, just as Randal's outstretched hand touched the boundary of the magic circle. The circle broke, and the col-

ored lights flared once and then died—but Gaimar's spell had already snapped into place.

Gaimar was laughing at Randal, as he had laughed so many times during their years at the Schola. "How do you feel now, Randy?" he asked. "The bell that you destroyed is whole again—and this time you won't get free so easily."

Randal stood unmoving, pinned between his fear of the spell Gaimar had cast upon Bell Castle, and his dread of the coming confrontation. Then a voice called out from the stairway—an oddly familiar voice, that spoke in the accent of Doun.

"Randal!" called the voice from the stair. "Randal, come out!"

Randal turned, and saw no one. When he looked back, Gaimar was gone. *He's used that medallion of his to vanish again*, Randal realized, *coming and going through his portal.*

"Randal—come out!"

Again, the voice. Randal went to the doorway and looked out. The stairway was dark, and the figure coming up the steps toward him was shadowed—all he could make out was someone of his own height, wearing a journeyman's black robe with the hood pulled up. The unknown journeyman extended a hand. Something metallic glinted from the palm.

"I knew I'd find you here," said the other. "Take this."

Randal reached out, and then stopped with his fingers just short of the piece of metal. "What is it?"

"The medallion Gaimar wore. It will take you to

the portal leading out of the castle. It's the only way out of here now."

Randal took the medallion on its thin cord. "Who are you . . ." he began, but the stranger had already turned and hurried away down the stairs in a swirl of black robes.

Thunder boomed outside the castle. Randal clenched his fist around the medallion and ran to one of Gaimar's glass-paned windows. He threw it open and looked out.

The tower that had fallen was now standing intact, and the bell was once more back in its place. Randal's lips tightened. *Lightning brought it down before,* he thought. *So lightning can do it again.* He gathered power to him and raised his hand—and as he did so, he felt the presence of another wizard on the other side of the courtyard, gathering strength even as he was.

We'll join our strengths, then, and knock down Gaimar's accursed bell with a double stroke.

Twin lightnings flew from the workroom window and the courtyard below, and once again Randal saw tower and bell fall and crumple into floating dust and jagged shards.

I was down in the courtyard, he realized, *and I was here in the workroom as well, after Gaimar's spell started everything in Bell Castle turning backward to what it was before—even the time, so that I can stand here in the present and there in the past at the same time. And it was my doubled strength that brought down the tower, when I cast lightning at the bell from two times at once.*

The medallion was cold and hard-edged inside

his fist. He opened his hand, and slipped the loop of cord around his neck beneath his tunic, so that the small disk of metal lay against the skin of his chest. Then he started down the stairs, half-fearing what he might find when he reached the bottom.

I have to get us all clear of Bell Castle while there's still a way out, he thought. *Danna said I had a little time . . . but how much?*

IX.

Duel

AT THE FOOT of the stairs, Randal stopped to strengthen the illusion that would keep him unnoticed in the crowded hall, and then stepped forward. The combat between Sir Reginald and Sir Guillaume was still going on. Randal heard the fighting before he saw it—the noise of heavy steel swords chopping against wooden shields in a broken, irregular rhythm—and then the crowd of onlookers shifted slightly, giving him a clear view.

Sir Reginald and Sir Guillaume still faced one another in the center of the great hall. Both men—Guillaume in his feast-day finery and Reginald in his dirty linen undertunic—were bleeding from nicks and slashes that armor, had they been wearing it, would have stopped. But where Sir Guillaume still appeared fresh and unwearied, his movements quick and agile, Sir Reginald was plainly weakening;

he moved more slowly than his opponent, and favored his wounded side.

There's fresh blood on his tunic, thought Randal. *He's opened up the wound he got during the fighting at the gate.*

Sir Guillaume brought his blade slashing forward in a blow that would have been lethal if it had connected. Randal held his breath, fearing the worst. But Sir Reginald's shield rose in time to deflect the glittering weapon, and a shout of appreciation rose from the crowd.

Randal wasn't fooled. Fess's men might appreciate Sir Reginald's fighting ability, but that meant nothing. If the castellan fell, nobody in the great hall would come to his aid. And sooner or later, Sir Reginald would fall. His skill was equal to Sir Guillaume's, or nearly so—but he was weakening, and giving way step by step before his enemy's attack.

I can't help him, either, Randal thought. *If I do, I'll call attention to myself, and lose any chance I've got of getting Walter and the others out of here alive.*

In the center of the great hall, Sir Guillaume's blows came faster and faster. Each time, Sir Reginald blocked the other's sword with his shield—but each time, his response was slower. Then Guillaume struck again, and this time Sir Reginald's shield wasn't there. The edge of Guillaume's sword cut into Sir Reginald's leg, and the castellan went down, bleeding heavily. Still he did not cry out, but raised his sword before him, as if to ward off the final blow that he knew was coming.

Guillaume swung his sword back behind his head, and snapped it forward in an arc. The blade came partway around, and then another swordblade blocked its swing—the long, heavy blade of a two-handed greatsword, as a man stepped out of the crowd and brought his own weapon into the path of the death-blow.

A familiar voice rang out in the feast-hall. "You would strike a wounded man on the ground? I really do believe that you would strike a man from behind as well."

Walter, you idiot, thought Randal as he watched the carefully cast illusion of vagueness fade under the gaze of the assembled crowd. Now his cousin stood before Fess and Thibault in his natural form. *How am I going to get us out of here now?*

Randal thought briefly of using magic to aid Walter. Then he shook his head. *I'd destroy my own disguise doing it—and something that drastic would probably bring Gaimar in here after me. I'll just have to trust Walter to know what he's doing, and work on getting Sir Reginald onto his feet and away from here without anybody noticing.*

Just the same, Randal feared for his cousin. Walter was surrounded by enemies, and facing a knight whose skill equalled his own. Worse, Walter was unarmored—and even if he won this fight, he would have to face another opponent and another until weariness made him falter.

They'll give him single combat, and call it honorable, Randal thought bitterly, *and then brag afterward about how one of their number brought down a hero single-handed.*

In the center of the feast-hall, several yards away from Sir Reginald's crumpled form, the two knights circled and eyed one another. Walter held his

110

greatsword two-handed before him, its five-foot length angled to point at Sir Guillaume's face.

"All right, now," he said to Guillaume. "Let's see if you can defeat me from in front."

Guillaume snarled at him over the edge of his shield. "I should have killed you when I had the chance."

"You tried, and even that you botched."

"It wasn't my fault that you didn't die," said Guillaume. "You were just a little slow in going about it, and then that cousin of yours interfered. Now your time has come."

"Kill me, then," said Walter with a short laugh. "If you have the strength and skill."

Randal pulled his attention from the fighters with an effort, and looked at the men-at-arms who lined the walls of the long room. No one had dared come too close to the fighting—there was too much danger of getting in the way of a blow—but not a single pair of eyes looked at anything but the circling knights. A few of the men had even climbed up onto the benches and tables for a better view.

Single combat is like a cockfight to them, or a bearbaiting, Randal realized. *This is probably the best wedding entertainment they've ever seen. And no one is watching Sir Reginald. If I'm going to help him, it'll have to be now.*

Still wearing his own illusion of vague resemblance to somebody who belonged among the crowd, the young wizard moved slowly forward. Nobody noticed him edging his way through the press to stand over the fallen knight. A quick glance showed him that Sir Reginald was still alive, though barely breathing.

I have to get him out of here, Randal thought. *But it's going to be tricky.*

At that instant, the two fighters ceased their circling and sprang into action. Guillaume stepped forward, and aimed a blow at the crown of Walter's head, his sword coming down in a silvery blur. But Walter raised his greatsword even faster to block the attack, and Guillaume's blade sprang back from the impact with a metallic, vibrating crash.

As part of the same movement, Walter spun away toward Guillaume's sword side. The greatsword whistled as it arced through the air—only to catch at the last moment on the edge of Guillaume's shield and swing away in another arc. The men who filled the feast-hall gasped as one at the narrow escape.

The duelists fought on. In spite of the deadly earnest of the combat, Walter wore the same calm but intent expression Randal had seen time and again during sword practice at Castle Doun, and he made the heavy steel greatsword move through the air with lightness and grace. Guillaume's face, by contrast, was caught in a grimace that made him seem to grin at some inner joke—but he, too, moved with a kind of deadly elegance.

The onlookers in the feast-hall, experts themselves in the art of swordfighting, had by now given the two men their whole attention. Some began to cheer the fighters along, pounding their mugs or the handles of their knives against the tables as they shouted. Even Fess and Thibault had come forward to watch, moving away from the false Lady Blanche—who still stood where Randal had cast the illusion minutes before.

Nobody, in all the uproar, had a glance to spare for the unmoving form of Sir Guillaume's defeated opponent. Randal lifted Sir Reginald to his feet. At the same time, he cast a spell to create an illusion of Sir Reginald lying on the floor, and extended his own disguise to cover the actual man. It was ticklish work, juggling so many spells at once—and not allowing the illusion of Lady Blanche to fade while he did it—but the spell casting went off without trouble.

It's a good thing the Prince of Peda liked stage plays, Randal thought. *Without all the practice I got in his theater, working with distractions and illusions, I wouldn't have been able to do this.*

He slipped an arm under Sir Reginald's shoulder, and—using a levitation-spell to support the weight of the wounded knight—started for the door that led to the courtyard. No one stopped them as they made their way through the lines of watchers; everybody's attention was fixed on the combat behind them.

Finally, Randal reached the threshold with his burden. The courtyard was empty, full of an eerie, echoless silence, and the bell tower stood unbroken above it. The sun still hadn't set, but stood unmoving in the sky at the point it had reached when Gaimar's spell took effect.

Then Randal saw with dismay that the courtyard

was not completely deserted after all—Lys and Blanche stood together on the steps just outside the open door.

"What are you two still doing here?" Randal demanded. "I thought you'd have had the sense to be gone by now."

"And leave you behind?" asked Lys. "Not likely." She paused, and nodded at the limp form of Sir Reginald. "Besides, Lady Blanche wouldn't go without her husband."

Indeed, the fight going on inside the great hall could be clearly seen and heard from where the group stood. Walter had backed Guillaume up almost to where the false Blanche stood with Fess and Thibault. Now, as the crowd howled, Guillaume threw a blow at Walter's unarmored side. Walter stepped back to let the swordblade pass harmlessly by, and spun the long blade of the greatsword around toward Guillaume's head before the Duke's champion could recover.

Too late, Guillaume saw the blow coming and only saved himself by lifting his shield up flat above his head. The greatsword took the shield on its center rather than on the rim, and split it inward. There was a loud crack as the shield broke—and Guillaume's arm, caught in the shield-straps behind it, snapped as well.

Guillaume went pale and cried out. He stumbled backward, his left arm hanging limp.

Walter brought the greatsword back up to the guard position, with the long blade held at the vertical before him. "Your arm is broken," he said. "Yield."

Guillaume stood looking at him for a second. Then the features of the Duke's champion contorted with rage. "Never!" he screamed, and threw himself forward into a wild attack.

As fast as Guillaume moved, Walter moved even faster. The tip of the greatsword whipped down and around, almost scraping the floor as it swung. It passed beneath Guillaume's blade and came up to catch the Duke's champion in the side, lifting him off his feet with the strength of the blow. In the same unbroken sweep of motion, Walter pulled back on the greatsword to free the blade, and Guillaume fell dead to the floor.

Walter came back again to guard. Blood coated his greatsword from point to grip, and more blood spread out from Guillaume's body in a red slick across the floor. Walter looked at Duke Thibault across the crimson pool.

"Do you have any more champions?" Randal's cousin asked evenly. "You know me, I believe—I am Sir Walter of Doun, and I won a ransom of you at Tattinham that still goes unpaid."

Nobody in the feast-hall moved.

Nobody dares, thought Randal. *Walter and that greatsword together are just too dangerous. It would take six good fighters all rushing him at once to bring him down—and the first five of them would die.*

Duke Thibault looked back at Walter for a long time without speaking. Finally, the duke nodded.

"I remember you," Thibault said. "And I grant

115

you the ransom you earned at Tattinham: You have safe passage out of this hall, as long as you leave me with my bride."

"The one you have beside you, you may keep beside you," said Walter. "And may you have the joy of her."

Slowly, as Fess's men looked on in silence, Walter backed away step by step down the hall, and passed through the great double doors into the courtyard. At a nod from Randal, Lys and Lady Blanche swung the doors shut behind him.

Walter lowered his bloodstained sword and looked at the group on the steps. "Everyone here?"

"Just waiting for you," Randal said with a smile. "What kept you?"

"Unfinished business," said Walter. He glanced up at the bell tower, looming unbroken above the castle walls. "I thought I saw that thing come down once already," he said. "Randy, you're the wizard— what's going on?"

"Gaimar cast a spell that's gotten out of control," said Randal. "We can't do anything but try to make it out the postern gate before the magic becomes so firmly fixed that nobody can leave."

"Right," said Walter. "Let's go."

The group hurried across the courtyard and down into the dungeons of Bell Castle with as much speed as they could muster. Nobody came out to stop them; the entire castle seemed to be gripped by the same uncanny stillness that had filled the courtyard. At last they found the postern gate, and

Walter lifted the bar out of the way. Then he put his shoulder to the door, and it swung open.

The door opened into nothingness. The land was gone, the sky was gone, the outer wall of the castle was surrounded by a mist that was at once all colors and no color, a swirling, mind-deadening void.

"Hallo the walls!" Walter shouted into the mist. No echo replied. The mist was neither warm nor cold, and neither bright nor dark, but Randal found that he could not focus his eyes upon it. Very carefully, Walter pulled the door closed and turned to look at Randal.

"Cousin," he said, "I trust you with my life—but we should have found rocks and trees outside that door. And sky. Does this have anything to do with the other strange things I've been seeing?"

"What kind of strange things?" Randal asked curiously.

"Myself," said Walter, "standing on the steps of the great hall while I was fighting over by the gate. I thought it was some kind of illusion, or that I'd been mistaken, and I didn't pay it any heed. But then later I stood on those steps, and saw myself fighting by the gate. Now that I've opened that door and seen what's on the other side, I ask you—what is going on at Bell Castle?"

"I've seen things too," said Blanche. "Like the bell tower, standing again after I watched it fall. And more things that hadn't happened, and things that had, happening and happening again."

"It's Gaimar," said Randal. "He tried to restore the bell and its magic, but he failed. All he did was start everything in Bell Castle repeating itself over and over. The castle is outside of time, now ... none of its ordinary doors will do us any good."

"Are we trapped here forever?" asked Blanche.

"I don't know," said Randal. "There's one more door we can try. Lys, Lady Blanche—hold up Sir Reginald between you. Now link hands, everybody—I'm going to try something."

The others looked uncertain, but obeyed. Randal took Lys's free hand, and with his own right hand he gripped the medallion hanging around his neck. Then he spoke the spell of transport.

He felt a moment of dizziness, and then darkness surrounded them all. "Don't worry," he said quickly, before anyone could cry out. "I think I know where we are."

He called up the cold-flame. Its chill blue light revealed a small, square room hewn out of the living rock. A circle was carved into the solid stone floor— by the signs and symbols cut into the rock around it, a magic circle fixed permanently in place. A plain wooden door was set into one wall of the room, with more symbols carved into the wood. And stacked inside the circle were six ironbound wooden chests with heavy locks—the same chests that Walter and Randal had escorted north from Peda.

"Where are we?" Lys asked.

"In the chamber of Gaimar's portal," Randal said. "It's built into the foundations of the castle itself, and leads into the world outside the walls. It's how Gaimar and his men were able to steal the gold. The only way here is with this medallion—the charm carved into the door means that it can only be opened from the inside."

"Then why make a door at all?" Walter asked curiously.

"Because even a wizard needs a back door sometimes," said Randal. "Everybody stand in the circle with me. We're taking the wizards' way home."

The group gathered around Randal as he stood in the center of the circle. When everything was ready, Randal spoke the words of portal opening— and nothing happened.

He lowered his hand. *We're lost . . . the medallion doesn't work. But the stranger who gave it to me said that it was the only way out.* Then he shook his head and laughed under his breath. *I'm blind, that's what I am. I've known all along that the only two Schola wizards in Bell Castle were Gaimar and me. . . . I got the medallion from myself, and I have to be there to give it to myself or the act won't be complete, and I'll never really have it at all.*

He stepped outside the circle.

"What's the problem, Randy?" Walter asked.

"This medallion is the problem," he said. "I haven't given it to myself yet."

Walter looked at him. "That doesn't make sense."

"Yes, it does," said Randal impatiently. "A journeyman wizard handed me the medallion, but the only two wizards in Bell Castle are me and Gaimar. So Gaimar's time loop is still playing tricks with us— unless I give myself the medallion, part of me will be trapped here in Bell Castle forever."

"If you say so," said Walter. "What do you want me to do?"

"Hold the door open," Randal told him. "If it closes, I'll never get back in."

The door opened onto a long passageway lit with torches. Randal stepped through and hurried down the corridor without looking back. The passage ended in a spiral staircase going up. The sense of urgency that propelled him grew even greater, and he was taking the steps two and three at a time before he reached the top and the open air. He ducked through an archway and ran out into the open yard.

The uncanny silence of the courtyard had not altered—except, perhaps, to grow even deeper and more still. The sky overhead was the same late-afternoon blue, but it seemed flat and without depth, covering Bell Castle like the inside of a painted bowl.

Randal looked up. Yes, the bell tower was there, reaching up toward that lacquered sky. *Gaimar's spell succeeded in a way he didn't expect,* he thought. *Everything about Bell Castle is the same now as it was before . . . and it always* will *be the same, now and forever unchanging.*

"So you came back to meet me after all," called a voice.

Randal turned.

Gaimar stood on the steps of the great hall waiting for him. "I'm surprised you even had the courage to try."

And with that word, Gaimar threw a fireball at Randal.

Gaimar's aim had improved since they were ap-

prentices: The fireball hit Randal this time, instead of only singeing his hair in passing. But Randal, too, had improved in skill and power—and he had spent the years since they had last met on the road, with only his wits and his magic to protect him, not sitting in a cozy workroom. With the speed of long practice he called up a shield-spell, and the fireball splashed against it. The flames scattered to either side, scorching the flagstone but leaving Randal unharmed.

Randal didn't pause to relish the look of surprise on Gaimar's face. Before the last of the fireball had died, he called up fire of his own—the blue-white fire of the cold-flame, magnified into a dazzling explosion of light—and cast it at Gaimar with the sound of thunder.

Gaimar fell back a step as the thunder boomed, but the light and noise failed to distract him from the combat. He shouted out words of power, harsh syllables that struck against the walls of the castle like metal hitting stone.

A wolf—or something in the form of a wolf, but larger, with eyes that glowed like red coals—appeared in the courtyard between the two wizards. The creature growled, and the hackles on its massive shoulders rose as its muzzle turned toward Randal.

X.
Healing

RANDAL HELD HIS GROUND, thinking furiously. *This could be just an illusion—no real wolf would look and act like that—but Gaimar isn't subtle enough to invent so complex an illusion. So whatever it is, it's real. And if it's real, then illusions can fool it.*

Randal surrounded the wolflike creature with a cage of illusory steel bars. The wolf-thing snarled, and began pacing back and forth inside the unreal boundaries of its prison. Gaimar snapped out a phrase of dismissal in the Old Tongue, and the creature vanished, leaving the phantom cage empty.

Creating the wolf took energy, Randal thought. *Maintaining it took energy, dismissing it took energy. Doesn't Gaimar realize that he can't afford to drag himself down until he has no power at all?*

Gaimar spoke on, chanting now, and sprays of rainbow light flashed toward Randal from his outstretched hands. Randal pulled magical energy to him and called up a mirror of solid silver in the path of the multicolored beams.

Rainbows dazzled in the air of the courtyard as the beams of light reflected off the silver mirror. One of the colored rays glanced off the shining surface and flew back at Gaimar. It touched the wizard's arm, and he began to bleed.

The sight of his own blood seemed to enrage Gaimar. He called up one shock-spell after another, throwing each one with all the strength in his body. Some of them Randal dodged, others he deflected—but still they came.

He's wearing himself out this way, thought Randal as another of the massive bursts of magical energy struck the flagstone where he had stood a moment earlier. *That blow wasn't as strong as the one before it, and even less strong than the one before that.*

Then Gaimar, too, seemed to realize that his strength was fading. He lowered his hand and stepped back a pace. Randal sensed the magical energies shifting around him as the wizard of Bell Castle drew on the utmost depths of his power, to spend it all in one final crushing blow.

He's still strong enough to kill me, thought Randal. *If I let him.*

Before the other wizard could speak, Randal raised his arms and called out the spell of magical resonance—the same simple charm that he used to discover where magic might be. But this time he called up the resonance spell at his opponent's loca-

124

tion rather than his own, so that Gaimar would feel his own power even as he let it loose.

The massive outpouring of energy from Gaimar's own spell entered the resonance, echoed back, and then fed itself to a higher echo. Gaimar used the echoing energy to feed his own spell, and again it echoed back to him. Randal could sense the spell stretching, almost breaking from the raw force it contained. He drew again upon his own deepest reserves, to keep the resonance up, pouring his magical energies into the spell until the simple structure was filled to overflowing with magic.

Gaimar fell to the ground. A moment passed, but he didn't move. Randal hesitated, stepped up to the young man lying face down on the flagstones, and bent to touch him. *I didn't mean to kill him, only to stop him.* But Randal's fear was unfounded. The pulse in Gaimar's throat still throbbed under Randal's fingers. Gaimar was only unconscious. The wizard of Bell Castle had been struck down by the overwhelming echo of his own power.

Randal turned Gaimar over. As he'd already half-expected, the bronze medallion was hanging around his old schoolmate's neck. He took it, and left the courtyard without looking back. *I hope that the rest goes as I remember it's going to happen,* he thought as he entered the great hall. He pulled up the hood on his robe to hide his features, and cast the vague-illusion-spell on himself a second time.

His precautions turned out to be unnecessary. Inside the great hall, he found the men-at-arms still crowded back against the walls, while Sir Reginald

125

and Sir Guillaume circled one another in the middle of the open space.

So far, the time-loop is working the way I expected, thought Randal. *It's brought me back to the point where I got the medallion.*

Nobody stopped him, and he found the hidden stairway without any trouble. "Randal!" he called out at the top of his voice as he climbed the steps toward Gaimar's workroom. "Randal, come out!"

Nobody answered. Again, he called, "Randal, come out!"

At the second repetition, a young man of his own height, dressed as he was in a journeyman's robes, appeared at the workroom doorway. Randal held out the medallion to him.

"I knew I'd find you here," Randal said. "Take this."

"What is it?"

"The medallion Gaimar wore. It will take you to the portal leading out of the castle. It's the only way out of here now."

Randal dropped the piece of metal on its thin cord into his younger self's hand, then turned and hurried down the stairs. He ran as fast as he dared through the feast-hall and into the courtyard, and from there down into the dungeons, hoping that he would find Walter and the others as he had left them.

If only it isn't too late, he thought as he ran. *If only we can get out before we're forced to stay in Bell Castle and fight with Gaimar and Sir Guillaume forever.*

At last, there was Walter, sword at the ready,

holding the door. "Close it," Randal gasped as he squeezed past his cousin and into the chamber. "Quick, everyone, into the circle!"

They clustered around him, Walter with his weapon in hand, Lys and Lady Blanche supporting the wounded Sir Reginald. Randal paused, gathering strength—he had lost track of the number of spells he had cast since he had arrived in the baron's camp. Then he spoke the words of portal opening—and at once they all stood on a cool, grassy plain, and it was night, with stars and a moon. The six ironbound chests rested in a semicircle on the ground behind them.

Lys and Blanche lowered Sir Reginald to the soft turf. Randal sank to his knees beside the wounded knight, and bowed his head in exhaustion. *I have to heal him soon,* Randal thought. *Nothing's keeping him alive but the spells I cast this afternoon—and their power will end soon.*

But the young wizard was bone-tired after the long effort to escape from Bell Castle. His mind flinched away from enduring a major healing-spell's demands on his own body and spirit.

Soon, he thought. *Soon. But let me rest awhile.*

"Randy," Lys murmured at his elbow. "Look at the castle."

Randal had to struggle to lift his head. *What now?* he thought. *Haven't I done enough?*

He opened his eyes, and looked out across the plain. Only the tents and men of the baron's army remained to show that there had ever been a castle and a siege at all. The spur of rock where Bell Castle

127

had stood was bare. An owl, pale in the moonlight, circled the empty crag.

"Danna," whispered Randal. "I knew she was working her own magic outside the castle, but I didn't know she was doing something as powerful as this."

"What did she do?" asked Lys.

"I don't know exactly," said Randal. "It isn't one of the spells the Schola teaches. But until Gaimar himself brought her inside the walls, she couldn't do anything about Bell Castle. Now she has."

The owl flew toward them and drifted down, transforming into a woman as it touched the ground. Danna stood there, appearing as Randal had first seen her, a young woman with her russet-colored hair dimmed by the moonlight.

"It is over," she said. "My thanks, Randal, for your help—the siege is ended, and my people are safe."

Randal shook his head. "They may be safe, but Sir Reginald is dying of wounds he took in helping us to win free—and I don't know if I have the strength to heal him."

Danna looked over at where Sir Reginald lay, pale and still as a carved statue on a tomb. "Come home with me," she said to Randal, "and bring these others with you. Another old friend of yours is waiting for you at my cottage—among all of us, this man may find the help he needs."

Randal nodded, and pulled himself to his feet. Together he and Danna went into the woods, with Lys and Blanche following behind, and Walter carrying Sir Reginald. They left the gold behind them without a backward glance.

Only a few feet inside the treeline, they came to the narrow bridge over the stream, and then to the little stone house. This time, all the windows blazed with light. Danna opened the door and beckoned them to follow her.

Randal stepped over the threshold, then halted, half-convinced that his exhausted mind was playing tricks on him. There, sitting on a stool by the hearth and warming his feet like any other weary traveler, was Madoc the Wayfarer, the master wizard who had first shown Randal the wonders of true magic. The passage of time hadn't changed the northern wizard. Madoc still wore a tribesman's saffron-dyed tunic and kilted cloak of gray wool. His close-trimmed beard had only a few more gray hairs mixed in among the brown.

"Hello, Randal," he said in his deep, northern-accented voice. "You've come a long way from Doun, lad."

Randal found his own voice at last. "Master Madoc. I'm glad you're here." He gestured at where Walter had laid Sir Reginald down on the trestle table. The wounded man's face was pale and beaded with sweat. "Help him, please, Master Madoc—he's near death, and I don't have the strength to heal him."

"I can give you strength," Madoc replied, "but I never made the healing arts my study. You'll have to cast the spells yourself."

For a moment, Randal felt as if the world had rearranged itself without warning. *Madoc is the master wizard, and I'm the journeyman,* he thought. *How can I have knowledge that he doesn't?*

But Madoc had to be speaking the truth. Randal squared his shoulders. "We have to hurry," he said. "We didn't have the time for a true healing spell earlier, and now it's almost too late."

The two wizards took their places at either end of the table where Sir Reginald lay. Randal closed his eyes, took a moment to compose himself, and then began to speak the words of healing. With a master wizard's energies to steady him, he worked on closing the leg wound that Sir Reginald had taken in the fight with Guillaume. After the leg was sound, he began the work of knitting together the broken ribs and torn ligaments and healing all the cuts and bruises that covered the knight's body. And through it all, Madoc was there, supplying the power that Randal lacked, supporting and steadying him when he faltered.

At last, it was done. Randal collapsed into the room's single chair. Even with Madoc's help, the healing had taken longer than any he had ever performed. He was so tired that the room was blurry in front of his eyes, too tired even to move from the chair to someplace where he could lie down. He lowered his head to the table and slept where he sat.

Next morning Randal awoke, cold and cramped, to an empty room. During the night someone had laid him down on a pallet on the floor. He stood, and stretched. Then a small movement near the threshold caught his eye, and he saw that he wasn't alone after all. Sir Reginald was standing just inside the threshold. The knight's features were still pale from his recent wounds, but his expression was determined, and Randal realized that he must have been waiting there for some time.

The knight cleared his throat. "A word with you, Master Randal, before you go."

"I'm not going anywhere just yet," said Randal. "And I'm only a journeyman, not a master."

"But you are a wizard," Sir Reginald said. "And I have to thank you for saving my life."

The knight paused for a moment, and looked away, as if ashamed. "There's another thing, as well. While I was lying in that cell and waiting to die, I kept thinking about my life, and all the things that I had done that were not worthy of a knight. Then I heard your voice in the dark, and I remembered another time, and a stableboy whom I had beaten for the sport of it."

He stopped, swallowed hard, and then met Randal's eyes again. "Do you remember the night I'm speaking of?"

"Yes, Sir Reginald," Randal said quietly. "I remember it."

Sir Reginald knelt before the young wizard. "Then I must ask your forgiveness."

Randal felt hot embarrassment rise in his face. "I forgave you long ago," he said, and realized as he spoke that the words were true. "Please—please get up."

Sir Reginald shook his head. "There must be

some way that I can make amends and repay you for saving my life."

He won't be satisfied until I give him something to do, Randal thought. *But I'm not a master wizard, to send knights running off on quests at my lightest word.*

"I'm sorry," he said. "But I can't think of anything I need . . . except breakfast, if there is any."

"Outside," said Sir Reginald, rising to his feet. "The other wizard said not to trouble you, but to let you wake on your own."

Together they went out into the little clearing that surrounded Danna's cottage. Randal saw the others sitting beneath a tree. A white cloth covered with good things to eat lay on the ground in their midst. Lys and Blanche made room between them, and Randal and Sir Reginald joined the group.

Randal found that his magical efforts of the day before had left him hungry. He ate breakfast for a while in silence while the others talked. Walter, it appeared from the conversation, had already been back to the baron's camp—looking for somebody who could take charge of the recovered gold—and had found most of Dreikart's mercenaries safe in their tents.

"It seems," Walter said, sounding a bit puzzled, "that at the height of the battle inside the gates, they all heard war horns blowing the signal to retreat . . . but neither Dreikart nor the baron can remember giving the order."

Madoc chuckled. "If they heard war horns blowing retreat, then someone must certainly have given the signal."

"Someone," said Randal. He smiled a little, re-membering that Madoc had always excelled in the magic of sound and light. "It was you who called them out, wasn't it?"

Madoc nodded, and smiled in turn. "They are good men, most of them—no worse than others in their profession, at least—and they didn't deserve to be trapped inside Bell Castle once the circle closed forever."

"What *did* happen to Bell Castle?" asked Lys.

"Two things," said Danna. "The spell I cast on it from without, once its defenses were opened to me, and the spell cast on it from within, by Gaimar himself."

She went on, her face stern as a judge's. "For the good of my people, it was time that the castle went away. So I made it do so. Lord Fess's wizard, mean-while, desired that the castle return to what it had been before its protection broke—and that, also, be-came so. Now the castle and all in it are removed outside of this world, to remain forever in a place where time and age cannot touch them."

Walter shook his head. "That's a hard fate," he said. "Gaimar and Thibault were villains, true enough, and Sir Guillaume was a false friend and a turncoat besides—but all of Fess's men-at-arms?"

Lady Blanche turned to answer him. "They were glad enough to witness a forced marriage and swear it was done of my own free will," she said. "And when my husband lay wounded and dying, none of them came forward to give him aid. I'll shed no tears for them, Sir Walter—what was done was well done, if you ask me."

Randal looked up from the crust of bread he'd been toying with. "But even Fess and Thibault were right about one thing," he said slowly. "Brecelande needs a High King, to bring back one justice and one law. If you really are the last of the royal family, Lady Blanche, maybe you should come forward and claim the throne."

She started to protest, but Madoc smiled at her and shook his head. "That won't be necessary," said the master wizard. "There is someone with a better claim than hers—and the time has come to make that claim known."

He set down his flagon of cider. "Let me tell you a story. Some years ago, the High King of Brecelande had a baby daughter and many enemies. When he saw that his enemies had trapped him far from aid, he asked for help from one of his friends, who happened to be a wizard. 'My life is forfeit,' he said, 'but if you love me, keep my daughter safe.' So the wizard took the High King's daughter to the only place he knew of where she would be truly secure—"

"Tarnsberg?" asked Randal.

Madoc shook his head. "No. Even in Tarnsberg, men and women still struggle for worldly power. The High King's friend took the infant princess across the borders of Elfland, and there, by the laws of Elfland, she must remain until someone fetches her out."

Randal was quiet for a minute, remembering another story he had heard Madoc tell. "You knew the High King when he was just Crown Prince and Warden of the Northern Marches," he said, "and you were still a journeyman. Were you also the wizard who saved his daughter?"

Madoc looked regretful. "I did the best I could for my old friend," he said, "but even then I knew it wasn't enough. In Elfland, the infant princess was safe from those who had taken her father's life—but I had to leave her there, in the King of Elfland's keeping, and once a mortal man departs from the Fair Realm of his own will, he can never return."

"Then how can the princess return to claim the throne?" asked Lys. "If you can't go back—"

Randal fell silent again. *Madoc can't go back. But the true queen is in Elfland, and somebody has to bring her home.*

He shivered as memories began to rise up around him. *While I was still an apprentice in Tarnsberg, I dreamed that my magic brought back life and growth to a barren land. And when I was a journeyman in Widsegard, the ghost of Master Laerg said that I had an important task waiting for me. And only three nights ago, I dreamed of a crown discarded and left for me to find . . . a crown that must go to its rightful owner, or else the land will remain forever barren.*

He drew a deep breath, and faced Sir Reginald. "A little while ago you asked me for something you could do," he said. "And it seems there is a way you can help me, after all."

"Only name the deed," said Sir Reginald, "and it shall be done."

135

"Take Lady Blanche somewhere far away from Brecelande," Randal told him. "Go south to Peda—she'll be safe there, out of the reach of would-be kingmakers like Baron Ector. Ask among Prince Vespian's players for an actor called Vincente; he has the prince's ear, and will help you both for my sake."

Then Randal turned to Madoc. "You can't fetch the High King's daughter back from Elfland," he said to the master wizard, "but someone must. Show me the road I have to travel, and I'll go in your place."

"Good lad," said Madoc, smiling at him. "I won't deny that I came here planning to ask that very thing of you—but the road to Elfland is a dangerous one for the unwilling heart, and it speaks well for your chances that you offered unasked."

Lys and Walter looked at each other, and then at Madoc. Lys was the first one to speak. "He doesn't have to go there alone, does he?" she asked. "I've heard too many stories about what happens to travelers in places like that."

"So have I," Walter said.

"Are the two of you offering your companionship freely?" asked Madoc. "Most of what you've heard about Elfland is lies, but this is the truth: No one who enters it leaves unchanged."

"Maybe," said Walter, and Randal saw that his cousin was wearing his stubborn expression again. "But the wizard Balpesh once told us that our lives and Randal's were entwined together, so that we shared the same destiny. If he goes, we go."

"Walter," said Randal. "Lys. You don't have to do this."

"Yes, I do," said Walter. "This is the good of the kingdom we're talking about . . . if I can do anything at all to help you, I'm honor-bound to try."

Lys nodded. "He's right, Randy. Do you remember, when we were in Peda, I said that the story wasn't finished yet—there was still something waiting for me in Brecelande? Well, I think this quest of yours is what I came back for."

Randal had to look down for a moment, to blink away the wetness that came to his eyes. "I don't deserve such friendship . . . you honor me, both of you. But if you're determined to make the journey, I'll be glad of your company along the way."

Master Madoc looked at Randal and his friends with grave approval. "So be it," he said. "Wizard, warrior, and bard . . . the road to Elfland awaits you."

Read the next exciting book in the series

CIRCLE OF MAGIC ⑥

HIGH KING'S DAUGHTER

by Debra Doyle and James D. Macdonald

A battle for the throne . . .

For as long as Randal can remember, Brecelande has been a kingdom without a ruler. Princess Diamante, the true heiress to the throne, has been hidden in Elfland, unable to return to her own world until the spells that guard her are broken.

Now Randal, Lys, and Walter begin their most important mission of all: to rescue the princess and restore her to the throne. Entering the magical realm is not easy, even for a wizard. But more dangerous still are the battles that await Randal and his friends in Brecelande. For Lord Hugo de la Corre has declared himself High King, and unless he can be stopped by Midsummer's Day, chaos will reign.

ISBN 0-8167-6997-4

Available wherever you buy books.